The
Ptomaine

A Hamburger
Western
Kid

The
Ptomaine

A Hamburger
Western Kid

Conger Beasley, Jr.

SUNSTONE
PRESS

SANTA FE

Sunstone books may be purchased for educational, business, or sales promotional use.
For information please write: Special Markets Department, Sunstone Press,
P.O. Box 2321, Santa Fe, New Mexico 87504-2321.

Book and Cover design › Vicki Ahl
Body typeface › ITC Benguiat Std
Printed on acid-free paper

Library of Congress Cataloging-in-Publication Data

Beasley, Conger.
     The Ptomaine Kid : a hamburger Western / by Conger Beasley, Jr.
        p. cm.
     ISBN 978-0-86534-905-6 (softcover : alk. paper)
     1. Cooks--Fiction. 2. Hamburgers--Fiction. I. Title.
     PS3552.E175P79 2012
     813'.54--dc23

                              2012029173

WWW.SUNSTONEPRESS.COM
SUNSTONE PRESS / POST OFFICE BOX 2321 / SANTA FE, NM 87504-2321 /USA
(505) 988-4418 / ORDERS ONLY (800) 243-5644 / FAX (505) 988-1025

Preface to the New Edition

*T*he *Ptomaine Kid: A Hamburger Western* was first published in 1981. There were some good things about the book; it was funny, offbeat, and inventive—redolent of the manic, creative spirit of the 1960s. In retrospect, it is also evident that the book was marred by many of the mistakes a young writer inevitably makes when he's not in full command of his vision and talent.

Few writers have the opportunity to revise an early work in hopes of making it better. This new edition of *The Ptomaine Kid* enables me to present a more compact, streamlined, and readable version. I am deeply grateful to James Clois Smith, Jr., editor and publisher of Sunstone Press in Santa Fe, New Mexico, for making this possible.

The Ptomaine Kid, like all books, is a product of its time. Many of the original edition's contextual references are dated and passe. Readers will quickly realize that in both tone and content the book evokes another time, another era. There are no references to cell phones or e-mail in these pages. The automobiles are different, the clothing, the food. A native Arizona people, the Tohono O'odham, are referred to as the Papago. The threat to the environment, an outbreak of ptomaine poisoning in the hamburger parlors of the American Southwest—the device that drives the plot and challenges the characters—seems benign when compared to the specter of planetary climate change we face today.

I look back nostalgically at the 1960s and 1970s as (possibly) the last great flowering of truly imaginative and experimental fiction in American letters. Richard Brautigan was still alive; so were Donald Barthelme, James Purdy, William S. Burroughs, Kurt Vonnegut, and Terry Southern. Cold War tensions between the United States and the Soviet Union continued to polarize the world, as they had since the 1940s; but by the 1960s we knew the enemy intimately and had developed a variety of satirical postures to counter the threat of nuclear annihilation. If the politicians and military honchos lost control and pushed the wrong buttons, the writers and movie makers and other protestors did not; it was their steady, dogged, defiant persistence in the face of atomic oblivion that helped make the difference. Today, we face a far more pervasive and insidious threat to our collective well-being in the form of global warming, and what role the creative artists of the world will play in dealing with this dilemma has yet to be decided.

—Conger Beasley, Jr.

for Jim Andrews
1936–1980

"The towheads were crazy about hamburgers. And so was his wife, for that matter. You could tell it, even if she didn't say anything, for she would lift her bowed-forward head a little, and her face would brighten, and she would run her tongue out to wet her lips just as the plate with the hamburger would be set on the counter before her. But all those folks, like Jeff York and his family, like hamburgers, with pickle and onions and mustard and tomato catsup, the whole works. It is something different. They stay out in the country and eat hog-meat, when they can get it, and greens and corn bread and potatoes, and nothing but a pinch of salt to brighten it on the tongue, and when they get to town and get hold of beef and wheat bread and all the stuff to jack up the flavor, they have to swallow to keep the mouth from flooding before they even take the first bite."

—Robert Penn Warren,
"The Patented Gate and the Mean Hamburger."
The Circus in the Attic and Other Stories (1959).

1

Hoby didn't like the mountains. He preferred unobstructed vistas, mountains behind or to the side, a view that started at his feet and swooped to the horizon. When his car was acting up, the engine pinging, he liked the mountains even less.

Usually the journey from San Diego was an easy three-hour jaunt. Up the San Bernardino Freeway to Temecula, east on state Route 74, down the dizzy face of the Santa Rosas, into the sandy bowl of the Coachella Valley. The Buick Skylark was eleven years old and showing its age. The fan belt screeched; the right front wheel clanked and wobbled. The car had accumulated more than 150,000 miles and for the past year had bled his pocketbook dry. "Just get me down off this mountain," he whispered, "and I'll treat you to a new fan belt and a lube job."

He breathed easier after making the turn at Paradise Valley. From there it was mostly downhill to the lower desert. If the engine conked out, he could coast the rest of the way. To his left rose a hillside of jumbled rocks, yucca stalks sticking out between them.

Hoby steered the car off the asphalt and onto a ledge perched high over Deep Canyon. A regular turnout on the twisting road, offering a spectacular view of the canyon, the slopes on the other side rising in steep tiers to the summit of Santa Rosa Mountain. A hot wind chapped his face. Squatting next to the right front tire, he sniffed the sharp smell of grated metal.

He brushed his fingers across his dry lips and stood up. That's when he saw it. Someone, most likely a hiker down into the canyon, had left a trail marker next to the trunk of a piñon tree, a neat stack of stones indicating the path of descent. He stepped closer. It wasn't a marker. It was a round, furry object with a stout beak and two smoky yellow eyes—an owl, most likely, maybe a foot tall, minus the claws and wings.

"Hey there, fella!" he called. "Who are you?"

The creature didn't twitch. Hoby poked a twig against its chest. It didn't budge or blink.

Hoby forgot about the car, the fading light, the business deal that had fallen through in San Diego. He crept closer to the creature. "There,

there, little fella," he murmured. "I won't hurt you. I just wanna find out who you are."

The eyes didn't blink, the head stir, or the feathers—if that's what they were—ruffle. Hoby lowered himself to his knees. The creature's beak was short and stubby, a triangle of gristle or bone. Hoby leaned forward and touched it with the forefinger of his right hand. He thought he felt something, a dull buzz that rippled up and down his arm. The sensation was warm and pleasurable. Hoby giggled. What kind of bird are you? he wondered. When he touched the creature with his left forefinger, he felt the same sensation. "So how did you get up here if you can't fly?" he muttered to himself.

The gaze that stared out from those remote yellow eyes was as deep as the canyon that plunged out of sight a few feet past the piñon tree. This close the oval eyes were cored with steely black pupils. The body felt solid and heavy—the body of a mammal rather than a bird. A steady heartbeat thumped through the fluffy down cloaking the body—a slow, throdding pulse, different from the rapid chitter of a bird. Hoby pulled off his shirt and wrapped the sleeves around the creature and carried it to the car, propping it up in the front seat. All the way down the mountain, as the front wheel thumped and the fan belt whined, Hoby stroked the creature and spoke to it softly.

2

The business venture that fell through in San Diego marked yet another effort on Hoby's part to raise the necessary capital to finance his own hamburger parlor. He had picked the location in downtown Indio; years of working as a cook in hamburger joints all over the Coachella Valley had endowed him with legendary skills. All he needed to realize his dream—a modest shop with a half-dozen tables, a counter with six or eight stools, quality service, fabulous burgers—was $25,000 down on the property plus a little more for the grill, a refrigerator, a dishwasher, say, $20,000 additional. But nobody was willing to take a risk—not the bank, not the savings and loan, not the jerk in San Diego who turned him down because the deal was too small.

The problem was collateral, or lack of it. With no tangible assets other than a creaky old Buick Skylark and a few securities totaling less than $20,000, Hoby didn't stand a chance of getting the loan he wanted. He was forty-one years old, divorced, with no children. He had deliberately avoided owning anything of real value during his life, preferring mobility and independence from financial entanglements. For fifteen years his father had called him a fool to his face, and now, when Hoby needed the money, he couldn't squeeze a nickel out of the old man. Randolph Tibbs had more than enough, but his principles would not permit him to loan anything to anyone who had so persistently and defiantly flaunted the rules of the American money-grubbing game. For twenty years, ever since he graduated from San Diego State University, Hoby had lived the life of an itinerant laborer—waiting tables, tending bar, picking grapes, frying hamburgers, caddying for rich golfers. Now that he finally wanted to open a business of his own, he would have to suffer. Randolph Tibbs was a great believer in dues paying as a prelude to financial solvency.

The wheel stayed on all the way to Indio. As the car chugged down the narrow lane into the date orchard, Hoby relaxed his grip. The clapboard duplex with the shake-shingle roof was located at the back of the orchard, screened off from busy Miles Avenue by a dense row of tamarisk pines. Elevated on concrete blocks to permit the air to circulate, the flaky green walls of the duplex merged with the darker green of the pines so that from the entrance on Oasis Street it was difficult to distinguish the two.

The orchard, located a few blocks from downtown Indio, was one of the few left inside the city limits. The others had been leveled to make room for developments, especially to accommodate the expanding Mexican American population. The orchard was owned by a wealthy forty-year-old widow named Amanda Rodriguez. In addition to owning property in the Coachella Valley, she was an internationally known vocalist. She had appeared in operas in San Diego, Caracas, and Guadalajara, although she was best known for her renditions of Latin American folksongs. A woman of beauty and power, she was a celebrated personality in the Mexican end of the valley.

Inside his half of the duplex, Hoby unraveled his shirt and propped the creature up on the bureau in his bedroom. During the journey down the mountain, the creature hadn't stirred or blinked or uttered a sound. Hoby pressed his thumb against its chest. A subtle vibration coursed along his wrist and jangled against his shoulder joint. Under the vibration, at the point of his finger, he could detect the steady thunk of a heartbeat.

After opening a beer and dumping a can of soup into a pot, Hoby telephoned his father. The old man sounded drunk but cordial. He agreed to see Hoby the next afternoon at 2:00, before Hoby had to report for work at the WhammyBurger franchise in Palm Desert. Hoby devoured the soup and drank another beer. Then he took some lettuce from the fridge and held it up to the creature's face. The creature didn't stir.

Tulio knocked on the door and shouted Hoby's name. Hoby didn't want Tulio to see the creature, so he tucked it inside his bedroom closet and stepped outside. On the grassy plot surrounding the duplex, they sat down on a pair of flimsy lawn chairs.

"How did it go, man?"

"Not so good."

Tulio, his wife, and daughter lived in the other half of the unit. Tulio tended the orchard, nurturing the date crop that sprouted in grape-like clusters under the wiry palm fronds. For this he earned a paltry wage and no medical benefits.

"No money forthcoming, eh?"

"Not from that source."

Tulio clasped his long dark fingers together. "What you gonna do, man?"

"I'm gonna speak to my father tomorrow. If that doesn't work . . . I don't know."

"We got a problem here too, man."

"What's that?"

"The widow. She thinking about selling this place to a developer from San Bernardino."

A ball of ice formed in Hoby's throat.

"It's true. I heard it last night in Patencio's. Where we go live then, man, if she squeezes us out?"

"I don't know. Rent in this valley is outrageous."

"I can always go in with Fiona's parents in Coachella. But shit, I don't care to do that. This orchard is my home, man. It has been for four years, ever since we got married. I don't ever want to move from this place."

Hoby settled his chin in his hands. Under the canopy of date palms, the light from the fading sun lit up the tight crosshatch pattern of the squat, thick trunks. Grapefruit and lemon shrubs grew in the irrigation troughs between the fig trees. Aligned in straight rows spaced fifteen feet apart, with citrus bushes filling the gaps between, the orchard formed a self-contained unit, an oasis of order and repose.

"You like to smoke a joint, man?"

"Nah. I'm too depressed, Tulio."

"Me too. What will I do if I can't harvest the dates, man?"

"You can go someplace else and harvest them."

"But this place, even though it isn't mine, it feels like it. I know every one of these trees. I love to climb them and look around. I belong in these trees, man. They make me feel good. I push my head up through the leaves and look out on the whole world. I know what they are feeling."

Hoby was bushed. He said goodnight and went inside. He tried to read, but the words made no sense. He watched television for a few minutes, then switched it off. He drew the creature out of the bedroom closet and held it to the light from the bedside lamp. The body was covered with a dark, downy pelt that felt more like fur than feathers. There were no wings. The feet were shaped like a pigeon's—three talons in front and one in back.

Hoby held the creature up to his nose. A strong, gamy smell tickled his nostrils. He turned it on its side and searched the underneath parts for a hint of its sexual identity. The humming sensation from its body flowed up and down his arms. Despite fairly detailed probing, he couldn't find any sign of genitalia.

"I think I'll call you Otis," he said, placing the creature on the window sill so it could gaze through a gap in the tamarisk pines at the Little San Bernardino Mountains north of Indio.

"Goodnight, Otis," he called a few minutes later as he slipped under the covers. The yellow eyes were clearly visible in the darkness of the shabby room, but Hoby was not discomforted by them.

He might have been puzzled, however, had he peeked under the blanket and seen how his fingers glowed in the dark, as if they had been dipped in a solution of liquid gold.

3

The next morning he carried Otis into the kitchen and placed him in an empty liquor box and put the box on the counter next to the sink. He shredded some lettuce and half a carrot and sprinkled them at Otis's feet. Then he tore up a slice of pressed ham and added it to the mix, along with a cup of water. Before leaving, he positioned the box so Otis could see over the rim and out through the kitchen window.

Tulio followed him downtown to the Buick dealer. The car sounded like a tank with a broken tread. Hoby clucked his tongue against his teeth. The tab for this repair might very well deplete the last of his dwindling reserves.

Tulio drove them back to the date orchard, then loaned Hoby his car to drive to Rancho Mirage to see his father. On the way, Hoby thought about the Widow Rodriguez. He had seen her twice, once on television and once in Buddy Patencio's bar in Indio. She was an attractive woman. Tall— taller than Hoby—with a curvaceous bust, slim neck, high cheekbones, warm brown eyes, and a coif of luxurious hair. A statuesque woman with a hearty coloratura chuckle and a captivating way of tilting her head back when she smiled.

Was she really going to sell the orchard? It didn't seem possible. Somehow he had to prevent that from happening. He and Tulio had friends. Although indistinguishable from countless other Anglo and Hispanic laborers in the valley, they were not without clout. If Hoby could just speak to her, he was positive he could convince her not to sell. Who knows, maybe she might see something in his eyes—his open, inquisitive, trusting face—that would appeal to her.

4

Randolph Tibbs lived in a trailer park in Rancho Mirage next to the prestigious Thunderbird Country Club. It was typical of Randolph that in his later years he would position himself next door to the type of neighborhood he had always aspired to but could never attain. However, that didn't dampen his ardor for his betters. Although he lived on a modest retirement income, years of observing the habits of the rich had endowed him with the same attitudes and mannerisms they possessed. He wore fancy golf clothes, even though he no longer played golf. He voted Republican, even though he believed FDR was the greatest president ever. He drove a Cadillac, even though it guzzled too much gas.

He greeted his only child with a sour grunt. His complexion was pale and blotchy, evidence of a hangover. He was nattily attired in yellow-and-white-checked slacks and a green Arnold Palmer golf shirt. He wore white leather slippers of Italian design, purchased in a snazzy men's shop in Palm Desert.

The trailer court was respectable. Landscaped walkways wound between the units. A security guard was posted at the entrance. From Randolph's front door he could see a portion of the ninth fairway of the Thunderbird Country Club. The sight of that manicured expanse, on which he was not permitted to set foot, filled Randolph with a curious satisfaction. Photos of famous golfers adorned the walls of his home. Every award he had ever won for anything, including a March of Dimes citation and a couple of bowling trophies, was displayed in a tall cabinet with glass doors. Randolph was proud to live in the same town as Gerald Ford.

After his wife died and he moved into the mobile home, Randolph decided to adopt a whole new look. Something casual and moneyed, totally at variance with the grubby, hardscrabble existence that had marked his years as the owner of a hardware store in Pomona, California. After reading several back issues of *Palm Springs Life*, Randolph decided that blue was the color most people with taste chose as the dominant motif in their homes. The carpet stretching wall-to-wall, from the front of the trailer to the back, was blue. The walls were powder blue. The blue lamps resting on the tabletops contrasted luridly with their Florentine gold bases. A blue spread, faded in spots, covered the circular bed at the back of the trailer.

"Well," Randolph began, firing up a filter-tip Doral and settling into a white vinyl recliner with his feet jacked up, "how'd it go in San Diego?"

"Not so good."

"He won't lend you the money, right?"

"That's about it."

"Something to do, perhaps, with the lack of collateral."

"That's correct."

"I thought so."

Randolph spoke with a lisp, a souvenir of his service in the South Pacific. Sitting in a foxhole on the island of Saipan one afternoon, he heard a voice say "Hey Yank!" He looked up to see a Japanese soldier not three feet away with a bayonet gleaming at the tip of his rifle. The soldier lunged and thrust the point of the bayonet through Randolph's cheek, spiking his tongue. Randolph's buddies jumped on the intruder and kicked him senseless, then emptied their weapons into his body. It took sixty-seven stitches and three shots of morphine to repair Randolph's cheek and tongue. The battle for the island was raging, and manpower was precious. Two days later Randolph was back in the field, his face black and swollen, working his carbine with deadly accuracy.

"I need the money, Dad. I know I've never wanted money before, but I want it bad now."

"Well, son, you know the terms."

"It's not fair, Dad. You can't punish me just because I want to open a business in an area you don't approve of."

"You can live where you like," said Randolph, tamping out the Doral in an abalone shell ashtray. "But no business bearing my son's name and backed with my money is going to be located in Indio, California. If you want to make a deal with me, you'll have to come up to this end of the valley."

"But the property up here, the overhead, is outrageous!" Hoby cried. "I can open a joint in Indio for the half the outlay it would take to get established here or in Palm Desert. You know that."

"Not only will you attract the right kind of customers at this end, but they'll have more jingle in their pockets."

"What have you got against Chicanos?"

"The same thing I got against niggers, chinks, and Filipinos. They belong in gardens and kitchens and behind washtubs."

"They work hard for their money. They appreciate good hamburger as much as anyone. And they're willing to pay a fair price."

"Son, that's tortilla and bean country down there. I don't have to tell you that. Beans and tortillas is what those folks want. It's what they been eating for thousands of years. Now if you want to open a tortilla and bean shop and call it Pepe's or Carlo's, then maybe we can talk business. But not hamburgers."

"Why not?"

"Son, let me tell you a little story. During the Depression, before you were born, a hamburger was considered by a lot of people, including rich folks, to be as good as a steak. Why, back then, if you could afford a hamburger you felt like a peacock. There wasn't anything better. I'd save up my dimes and nickels and go into a café and order a hamburger. Steak was way out of my reach. Hell, it wasn't until after the war that I was able to sink my teeth into one on a regular basis. But a hamburger was within range. To sit at a counter and smell one cooking on the griddle really activated my taste buds. And to have one dished up to me on a plate, and after I had doctored it with the right mix of garnish, why then to sink my chops into that concoction was a fabulous pleasure. For a few moments, for as long as it took me to chew it down, I forgot all about being poor and miserable. I was as rich as John D. Rockefeller. I was king in my own castle. I was chief of all the other Indians.

"And so, son, I'm all for you going into business for yourself. You're forty-one years old, and it's about time you settled on your life's work. But seeing as how you want to make hamburger that occupation, and seeing as how you need me to cough up the greenbacks, and seeing as how my philosophy toward hamburger is definitely elitist, you're gonna have to comply with my wishes to make the deal. A decent place up here at the white end of the valley, with a fancy interior and pretty waitresses with perky tits and a bar that serves beer and wine, and linen napkins. Don't forget the linen napkins, son. This is the Coachella Valley, playground of some of the highest rollers in America. People who can afford to come here and spend their time want to eat off fancy plates and wipe their lips with linen napkins. They may have spent the first thirty years of their lives eating with plastic spoons and wiping their lips with their sleeves, but for the next thirty they want to eat off china and dab their greasy lips with a piece of expensive material. Sorry, son, but that's a fact of life."

5

Hoby had always been fascinated by hamburgers. As a boy he used to help his father grill them on the patio. On the weekends his parents had people over, and they drank beer and danced to the songs on the radio and ate hamburgers. Pomona was a pleasant, pretty town back then, filled with citrus groves, mom-and-pop shops, docile Mexicans, old people with respiratory complaints from the steel towns in Michigan and Ohio who had moved to California to get well. In the heat of summer the grapefruit fields gave off a sweet, tangy scent. Kids rode their bicycles everywhere, followed by packs of friendly dogs. The air didn't get smoggy until late afternoon.

The patties looked delectable cooking on the grill. There was no filler in the meat, only 100 percent ground beef. The flavors exploded in Hoby's mouth, the meat mixing with tomato and lettuce and onions and a smear of Durkee's or French mustard. The buns were fresh; the meat dripped hot, sticky juice down his wrists. His parents' friends liked hamburgers too, especially the way Randolph fixed them. Packed thigh to thigh at the picnic table on the back lawn, they slurped and chawed and gulped. They wiped their greasy chins with the backs of their hands. They rinsed their throats with glasses of beer and bourbon. They talked, sang, told jokes, got drunk, and danced with each other's wives.

Hoby liked these parties. His parents let him stay up late and drink beer and eat hamburgers. "Eat up, son!" his father shouted. "We fought this war so we could eat all the hamburger we want!"

Sometimes Hoby ate so many hamburgers he had to be helped into the house. Belly swollen, eyes glazed, he waddled through the kitchen, guided by his mother who by that point was none too steady on her feet. The walls of his bedroom whirled around his head. The bed rocked like a boat in a high sea. He passed out remembering how his dad had let him turn the patties on the grill. The whole time his father drank steadily, I.W. Harper and water no matter the season, his scrawny rooster face flushing brighter with each glass.

Randolph sold nails and wrenches and pitchforks and galvanized buckets and garden trowels to the good people of Pomona. He was a shopkeeper, a small businessman, the backbone of the postwar capitalist economy. He'd never make a million, but then he wasn't supposed to. He was content simply to make a living. If it wasn't a fancy life, it was certainly sufficient. But that wasn't enough for Hoby. He wanted something different—a wildness, a sense of risk, an authentic connection. Randolph's life seemed too stodgy and predictable.

Like his father, Hoby could fry a mean hamburger. Some twist or turn or knack made it different. A sense of timing, the flick of a wrist, knowing when to remove the patty from the griddle, what ingredients to flavor it with. His skills were lauded all over the Coachella Valley. The WhammyBurger outlet in Palm Desert did the most volume of any in the region. Hoby was proud of his talent. Now, in his early forties, he wanted a portion of that gift for himself. For ten years he'd worked for a franchise, pleasing the masses as well as the big bosses. He was tired of it. He wanted his own place. He wanted to see his name in lights above the door.

6

We got troubles," said Deeter Jester, the manager of the Palm Desert WhammyBurger.

"What's up?"

"Five calls already from customers who've been poisoned by our hamburgers. Five freaking calls, and it's only 3:30 in the afternoon. We musta served forty-five hamburgers for lunch, and how many more are gonna call in sick?"

"I checked the new shipment that came in Friday, Deeter, and it looked okay."

"Yeah, but it isn't okay, Hoby. It's rancid. It's crawling with buggies that are upsetting the tummies of our customers. We can't afford that. The competition's too stiff."

Hoby marched into the kitchen and strapped on an apron. The morning cooks were about to go off duty. Hoby questioned them about the hamburger. Unlike the other franchises, WhammyBurgers did not arrive in Palm Desert in preformed patties. Hoby liked to make up his own patties according to the customers' wishes—thin, fat, in-between. Hoby let them choose, then he formed the patty with his hands, mixing the meat with flakes of onions, green pepper, cheese, a touch of garlic, a tangy Cajun seasoning. The hamburger took longer to prepare, but the customers loved it, and so Hoby had instructed the other cooks—with Deeter's approval—to do the same thing. The headquarters office in Riverside squawked at first but shut up after the Palm Desert branch outsold every other outlet in southern California.

"What did the hamburger look like when you took it out this morning?" Hoby snapped to an earnest college student from UC-Irvine, who was spending the semester learning the franchise business.

"It looked fine, sir. It looked normal."

"No different colors? No suspicious odors?"

"No, sir."

The other cook, an old-timer named Frank, who'd served on merchant ships crossing the North Atlantic during World War II, reported the same thing.

"What about when they were frying. Anything suspicious there?"

"Nothing," said Frank. "No problem. Pretty as a picture."

The student was nervous. The usually jovial Hoby looked grim, his mouth clenched.

Deeter had already called the WhammyBurger office in Riverside, fifty miles away. A man was on the way. Reluctantly and for the first time in twenty-three years in the short-order business, Deeter gave the order that no more hamburger was to be served until the cause of the outbreak had been tracked down.

Hoby opened the freezer and took out a box of hamburger meat. The box was the size of an ordinary liquor box, lined with wax paper. As Hoby swung the heavy box onto the counter, he felt his fingers shiver. With a spatula he scooped out a chunk and spread it across the counter. The hamburger looked fine—rich, red grains of glistening protein. Hoby shoveled out another load and added it to the pile. Then he plunged his hands into the meat . . . testing, exploring, feeling. The tips of his fingers tingled. An odd, crackly sensation. Hoby was puzzled. Frank and the UC-Irvine student looked on attentively.

The man from the Riverside home office arrived a few minutes later, a tall, balding man wearing a dark suit, gray tie, and horn-rimmed glasses. He took charge immediately, herding Deeter, the cooks, the dishwashers, and three of the five waitresses into the kitchen. "Ptomaines are chemical compounds related to ammonia," he began in a dull, schoolteacherish voice. "All of you have smelled ammonia at some time, so you know what I mean. Ptomaines are produced as waste products by bacteria that can cause decay or decomposition of organic plant matter. They bear some resemblance to the alkaloids found in poisonous plants and animals. In 1870 an Italian bacteriologist named Francesco Selmi introduced the word ptomaine, from the Greek *ptoma*, meaning 'corpse.'"

"Spare us the lecture, Ralph," Deeter groaned. "I got a business to run."

"There's a truck on the way," said Ralph with no shift in tone. "Everyone stay calm. If we pull together we can lick this thing."

Deeter was frantic. He'd already smoked a dozen cigarettes; his throat felt like an ant pile. "When did the truck leave?" he rasped.

"It pulled out a few minutes after I did. They radioed me on the CB. They ought to be chugging in here any minute."

Deeter was tall and thin, a former junior college basketball star from Illinois. When he got excited, he brought his hands up to his chest and flicked his eyes around as if trying to locate the whereabouts of an imaginary ball.

"They better, Ralph. I need that hamburger bad. It's a cutthroat business down here. We got new joints springing up every day. If I lose a customer he can always go down the street to Bob Keedy's."

"We in the Riverside home office understand your problem, Deeter. That's why I'm here to give you personal, effective service. You know my reputation."

On impulse, Hoby dumped the rest of the hamburger out of the box and combed it into a heap on the counter with the spatula.

"I wouldn't do that if I were you," Ralph cautioned.

Hoby ran his hands lightly over the glistening stack.

"You're exposing the microbes to a lower temperature, which could hasten the process of decomposition."

Hoby thought he could detect something moving inside the mound of hamburger meat. Something infintesimally small that under normal circumstances he shouldn't be able to detect at all. The tingling in his fingers intensified.

"Hey, Ralph, do you know who you're talking to?" Deeter asked.

"An employee of WhammyBurger, Inc."

"More than that, Ralph. You're talking to the best damn hamburger cook in the desert, maybe in all of California. This is Hoby Tibbs, and he knows everything there is to know about hamburger."

Hoby stared transfixed at the mound of grainy red meat. His body twitched, his hands jerked. There were spots grubbing underneath the pile. Hoby could see them. Tiny spots invisible to all other eyes without benefit of a microscope, coming alive in the warm kitchen air, stirring, ready to erupt at the application of the proper heat.

"Hoby," Deeter called. "You all right?"

"Something wrong here," Hoby muttered. An intuition pulsed through his brain like the track of a falling star. If he could see the microbes in the raw hamburger meat, he ought to be able to touch them. And if he could touch them, simply by the application of his fingers he ought to be able to heal them.

His hands twitched spastically. Electric jolts shot past his elbows.

"What's the matter with him?" Ralph asked nervously.

"Hoby!" Deeter hissed.

A peculiar intelligence seized possession of his fingers. Another intuition sparked his brainpan: why not run his hands through the pile of meat, squeezing the infected areas, rubbing them away?

Poised on his toes like a diver, he plunged his hands into the meat and began caressing it.

"Hoby . . ." Deeter took a step forward to restrain the madman when something stopped him: a look in the madman's eye, a glint of absolute certainty. Deeter came up alongside, curious, followed by Ralph and the others. "Hoby, you damn well better know what you're doing."

"I do, Deeter. I think I can spot the microbes. The meat is tainted. They're in there by the thousands. And they're starting to come alive."

"That's preposterous!" Ralph said.

"They're here . . . and here . . . and here . . ."

Frank felt the hair prickle on the back of his neck. The UC-Irvine student gasped out loud.

"I think that by touching them with my fingers I can make them go away."

"Deeter, I insist you call the police!"

"Take it easy, Ralph! Take it easy!"

Hoby stared down at his fingers. The tips were swollen and gave off a faint glow.

"I've never witnessed anything so preposterous in my life!" Ralph declared.

Hoby patted a clump of hamburger together and plopped it down on the counter. "Test it," he said. "You got the chemicals. Test it and see if I'm right."

Ralph pursed his lips indignantly.

"Do it, Ralph!" Deeter cried.

The staff crowded around. Ralph opened his briefcase and took out a plastic kit. Using a special dye from a bottle with a fluted neck, he sprinkled a few drops on the patty Hoby had formed on the counter. The clear, transparent dye turned white. Under the white coating hordes of unsavory specks congealed into view.

"Christalmighty!" Deeter shouted. "That's them, ain't it, Ralph? Them little black thingamajigs?"

It was Ralph's turn to gasp.

"Now watch this," Hoby murmured.

He scooped up the mound in both hands and began squeezing and massaging it. Then he formed the giblets back into a patty and laid it on the counter.

"Now test it again."

Ralph applied the dye, coating the entire patty. The dye turned white. No specks appeared.

Hoby broke the patty in half. "In there," he ordered.

Ralph did as he was told. The dye turned white. No dots or specks appeared. The patty was bug-free.

Ralph screwed the cap back on the dye and put the kit in his briefcase. "How'd you know to do this?" he said gravely.

"I'm not sure."

"You must have had a clue."

Hoby shrugged. "It was just a hunch."

"Ralph, you know what this means?" Deeter said. "It means that if he can cure that one little patty, he can cure the whole bunch. It means the solution to our problem is standing right here in this kitchen. It means we don't have to worry about any outbreak of ptomaine poisoning."

"It means," said Ralph, after clearing his throat, "that we can corner the market on clean hamburger."

7

Tulio was looking for a book in Hoby's half of the duplex. Hoby never locked the door, so Tulio came in through the kitchen and looked around the bookcase in the sitting room. The room was messy, and Tulio had trouble locating the title. He found it and stepped back into the kitchen. That's when he saw the creature. It was out of the box, perched on the ledge above the sink, staring out the window.

Tulio dropped the book and stooped hastily to retrieve it. The commotion failed to ruffle the creature. Tulio was surprised. A real bird or animal would have been frantic to escape. But the creature didn't twitch. The hairs across Tulio's back hackled up. His people were from Tucson and before that the mountains of Sonora. He was part Yaqui, and the creature's resemblance to an owl unnerved him. He swallowed hard and stepped across the kitchen floor. It wasn't an owl; it was something else—what he did not know. There were no wings, no tufted ears. The beak was flat and straight, the oblong eyes luminous and yellow. Tulio had never seen eyes like that before.

The creature did not show the slightest fear or concern. Tulio slipped closer, cutting across the linoleum floor at an oblique angle. The creature seemed utterly absorbed by the sight of the paloverde tree swaying in the desert wind outside the window. Tulio was puzzled. The creature was weird and otherworldly. There was nothing he could compare it to.

Slowly, not turning his back, Tulio stepped across the kitchen, out the door, into the disturbing glare of the afternoon sun.

8

It was the beginning of his power.

Lamar G. Whammers himself wanted an audience with Hoby. The next day, after the Buick was out of the shop, he drove up the San Gorgonio Pass to Riverside.

Hoby Tibbs had never laid eyes on L. G. Whammers. He had never seen his photo in the newspapers or society columns. He had never been to the executive offices in Riverside; he'd never had any desire to go. He had no idea how the company was run, along what corporate lines it was structured. Hoby was a burger man, a griddle chef, a patty maker, concerned with dishing up the finest possible eats, mouthwatering and scrumptious. The fact that the Palm Desert franchise was one of many did not bother Hoby. He wasn't interested in the big picture. The center of his universe was the griddle on which he served up to seventy-five hamburgers a day. He wasn't interested in statistics or plaques or special awards or executive citations. He was interested in hamburgers, how they were made and how they tasted. L. G. Whammers was just the name of the fellow who signed his checks.

The office was roomy enough to stable a dozen head of cattle. It seemed oddly appointed but in good taste. A burnt-orange carpet gave bouncily underfoot. Behind the desk, rising from floor to ceiling, hung the propeller of a P-47 Thunderbolt, a World War II-vintage fighter aircraft Lamar had flown in the Caribbean. At the far end of the room stood a conference table, surrounded by a dozen upholstered leather chairs. One wall was covered with glossy framed photos of political leaders such as Rafael Trujillo, Chiang Kai-Shek, Fulgencio Batista, and Anastasio Somoza. At the other end of the room, flanked by two brass spittoons, was a stand-up bar with a foot rail. Behind the bar hung a beveled mirror.

Whammers stood up as Hoby entered and came around the desk, walking with a vigorous gait, his right hand extended. The grip, for such a small hand, was hard and insistent. Hoby was surprised to discover that Whammers was shorter than him by a couple of inches. He had been pestered by the notion that a mogul the likes of Lamar Guston Whammers would necessarily be tall and imposing.

Lamar was attired in gray flannel trousers, a white Oxford cloth shirt, and a navy-blue blazer spangled with gold buttons. A subdued, affluent look indicating an East Coast orientation. The only California concession, a pair of silver bracelets banding his left wrist, jangled softly as the hamburger baron directed his most prominent chef to a chair in front of the solid mahogany desk on which were stacked papers and computer printout sheets.

Hoby had been briefed by Deeter Jester about Lamar's proclivity for sizing people up before launching into conversation. Lamar proceeded to do just that, lighting up a Canary Island cigarillo and leaning back in his chair and peering at Hoby through slit-like eyes. Hoby stared back. He was pleased by the close scrutiny. When a man looked at you like that, you knew he was going to ask you for more than just the time.

Lamar's face resembled a nicked and smudged softball. The nose was flat, the lips puffy, the forehead swept high over a lattice-work of intagliated wrinkles to the crown of a shiny bald skull. A deceptive face, with mobile features. The eyebrows, bushy and powdered with white hairs, formed fuzzy half moons over a pair of glinting blue eyes. An expressive face, full of charm and cunning. A face you couldn't quite trust yet wanted to.

"They tell me," he began, leaking tobacco smoke out of both sides of his mouth. "They tell me that you got some kind of magic power in your fingers."

The voice was soft, furry around the vowels. Southern in its slurry sentence endings: "Fin-gahs."

"I reckon so, Mr. Whammers. Though at this stage it's too early to tell how much."

Lamar pulled thoughtfully at the wet tip of the cigarillo. "A talent of the sort you've acquired is a most remarkable asset, Mr. Tibbs. An organization like ours, with scores of service outlets, could certainly make use of it."

"Ah . . . well . . . yes, sir."

"I'm going to let you in on a little secret, Mr. Tibbs, which only a handful of people in my organization know about. In recent weeks there's been a serious outbreak of ptomaine poisoning in both California and the Southwest. Not only has our chain been affected but others as well. The information I'm giving you, Mr. Tibbs, is strictly confidential. However, you look like the sort of man who can keep a secret. We don't know exactly what's causing this outbreak. We think it's related to something the cattle are eating, but we're not sure.

"Now as you know, Mr. Tibbs, from having worked with the

WhammyBurger chain, we use only the finest grade A chuck to make our patties. Even then we've not been able to control the spread of this terrible pest. We've had reported outbreaks of ptomaine poisoning in thirty-five of our sixty-one outlets here in California. I don't have to emphasize to you the severity of the problem. So far, we've managed to keep the word from leaking to the public."

Hoby shifted his weight in the chair and recrossed his legs.

"I propose that we enlist your God-given talent for curing tainted hamburger to rid the WhammyBurger chain of these microbes. I have here a detailed report from Ralph Manning, our Riverside County supervisor, describing your performance yesterday in the Palm Desert outlet. A most remarkable display of digital prowess, Mr. Tibbs, if I do say so myself. It seems to me that the two of us, working with both our interests at heart, could draw up a contract that would free you of your cooking duties and send you out on the road to those outlets stricken with the affliction. On a healing mission, you might say, an errand of mercy, and at a considerable increase in salary."

Hoby cleared his throat and shifted around in his chair. "Well, Mr. Whammers, I'll be straight with you. I love hamburgers. I love cooking them, and I love eating them. In fact, I doubt if there's anything in the world that I love so much as a properly cooked hamburger. It's to my taste buds what the sight of oil is to the eyes of an Arabian sheik. It's my desire one day to own my own hamburger stand. Oh, don't worry, I'm not going to run you out of business or even try and compete with you. I just want to open a little place down in Indio where I can serve hamburgers to people the way I like to cook 'em."

Lamar was puffing on his second Canary Island cigarillo, squinting hard at the man sitting across from him. Veils of gritty smoke fumed off the embered tip. The fellow wasn't easy to draw a bead on. Lamar was adept at assessing people's usefulness to him, but he couldn't quite get a fix on Tibbs. He sensed there was something incorruptible about him, an integrity so fundamental it couldn't be violated. A small man, compact, with dark steady eyes and delicately formed hands. Small hands for such a broad-shouldered man. Quick, alert, volatile hands, ready to erupt into action. Lamar was puzzled. But for the moment that wasn't important.

When he wanted something from somebody, L.G. Whammers was known to have the patience of an ox.

"Let's just say right now, Mr. Whammers, that I'd be delighted to go out on the road for you, but only on a per diem basis. I will sign no contract that will bind me to you for a longer period than the job takes. I want to do all I can for the hamburger industry of America, but I also wish to maintain my independence."

Lamar choked down the guffaw rising in his belly. "And what are the specifics of the deal you are proposing, Mr. Tibbs?"

"Well, sir, I propose to work out a schedule with your staff that would enable me to visit all the outlets that are currently in trouble. Then, as the malady is apt to recur, I'd like to set up a return schedule."

"Do you want to be paid by the job or by the day?"

"By the day, Mr. Whammers. Two hundred fifty dollars a day, plus expenses."

Lamar winced. "That's pretty stiff, Mr. Tibbs. I'll need some sort of guarantee that the job will get done."

"Look, Mr. Whammers, I've only done this once, and that may have been a fluke. How about we do a test run? Send me to three of your troubled outlets here in the Riverside area, clustered together so I can get to all three in a single day. The first three will cost you only two hundred dollars plus expenses. If I'm successful, we'll negotiate the price upward in my favor."

There was no guffaw in Whammers's belly at this proposal. This was nuts and bolts, the kind of language he liked to hear. Tibbs was a starchy sort, humorless, eager to obtain results. Lamar liked that. The two might have more in common than they knew.

9

Hoby was amazed at his own moxie. Two hundred and fifty dollars a day! He had no idea when he walked into Whammers's office that he would ask for that amount. He was even more astounded when he actually got it. Something in him had changed. His perception of himself as a marketable item had become a reality. L. G. Whammers was no patsy. The man hadn't become a hamburger baron by rolling over and playing dead.

Hoby floated out of the Riverside office on shaky knees. What a bolt of good fortune! If the magic remained in his hands for a hundred working days, he could amass $20,000—enough for a down payment on the hamburger stand in Indio.

The three franchises he had agreed to inspect were located in San Bernardino. Hoby returned to Indio, packed a few clothes, and drove back to a motel in Riverside. The next morning a staffer from the executive office drove him to the first franchise. Hoby was nervous. His palms were moist. He hoped that didn't impair his efficiency. How could he cure bad hamburger with wet palms?

The outlet was one of the older models, built in the 1950s. A stern, fortress-type design, with machicolated turrets at the corners like a medieval castle. Whammers's calculated nod to the festung mentality of the 1950s. America as a bastion of freedom against Communist aggression. Painted a dour, penitentiary gray with red, white, and blue trim around the doors and windows, only two of these structures had survived the onslaught of progress in southern California. They had recently been featured in an architectural review as notable examples of postwar American commercial schlock.

Accompanied by the staffer, Hoby marched through the door of the franchise at 9:30. All the tainted patties were piled on the counter. The cooks, busboys, and waitresses eyed him warily. They didn't like the idea of an outsider tampering with their stuff, especially a nondescript little man with fair skin and curly black hair, dressed in a dark cotton shirt and paint-spotted Sears work pants. A hamburger wizard was a person whose authority, like that of a Canadian Mountie, was obvious at a glance.

He barely nodded to the manager. "Anything you need, Mr. Tibbs, you just let us know," the man said, backing away.

Hoby had no plan. The sight of all those patties stacked on the counter was intimidating. There must have been a hundred of them, arranged in a truncated, Mayan-style pyramid. First he peeled off all the wrappers. Then he crumbled the patties into a mound of rosy hamburger meat. For the next forty-five minutes he moved his hands through the meat, grinding, kneading, squeezing. Once the pile had been thoroughly treated, he nodded to the cooks, and the three of them molded the shapeless mass back into patties. "That should do it," Hoby announced an hour and a half after walking into the place. The Mayan pyramid had magically reappeared, a two-foot stack of glorious hamburger ready for the grill.

The Riverside staffer ran a careful chemical analysis on the patties. The results were negative; no bacterial microbes were anywhere in evidence. Hoby had cured the meat.

"That's a miracle!" said a waitress.

"It damn well looks like it," the manager sighed. "But we'll let our customers' stomachs be the final test."

Hoby's chest swelled with pride. A shiver coursed the length of his arms from his fingertips to his shoulders. He lowered his hands gingerly into a sink full of suds. The warm water soothed his aching digits. The muscles relaxed, especially the sore spot between his thumb and forefinger. The Riverside staffer beamed proudly. As they walked out of the store, the entire crew lined up at the door to pat his arm and offer congratulations.

10

It was the same at the other two outlets. The crew was unfriendly when Hoby first appeared. A few wisecracks were uttered, which the Riverside staffer tried to gloss over with a smile. Hoby paid no attention. His success at the first outlet had given him confidence. His fingers hummed with energy. Let them scoff all they wanted, he thought. He had a job to do.

Lamar was delighted. Two days after the San Bernardino performance, there were no reports of food poisoning in the three outlets. He paid Hoby the amount agreed upon, then drew up a contract offering him $250 a day plus expenses to check on the other troubled outlets. With results like these, Hoby was a bargain. The WhammyBurger franchise sold millions of dollars of hamburgers every year. Not as many as McDonald's or Burger King maybe, but pretty darn close. According to every survey Lamar had taken, WhammyBurgers were favored over all others. They were tender, flavorful, juicier. Lamar had awards and citations from industry experts to back up his claim. Best of all were the testimonials from satisfied customers. Lamar had a file cabinet full of them.

So far, the ptomaine outbreak had been confined to California and the Southwest, where practically all the WhammyBurger outlets were located. If the plague continued and Lamar had to stop serving hamburgers, his organization's existence might be imperiled. Now, with the appearance of Hoby Tibbs, Lamar had acquired a valuable piece of insurance. Two hundred fifty dollars a day was nothing compared to the money Hoby could save the company by keeping it alive and pumping.

Three days after the San Bernardino episode. Lamar asked Hoby if he would go to northern California to work a few outlets up there. Hoby agreed, provided he could go alone, unescorted by a staff member. "I'm a loner, Mr. Whammers," he said. "I like to work by myself. I'm happier that way. Just pay my motel costs, my gasoline, and my dinner money, and I'll take care of the rest."

Whammers nodded. "Whatever you say, Mr. Tibbs. After your San Bernardino performance, you can write your own meal ticket."

Hoby didn't tell him about Otis.

11

In a fancy luggage store in downtown Palm Springs, Hoby bought a special carrying case. Tall and oblong with a zipper at the top and a loop handle, it looked like the kind of case a person might carry a bowling trophy in or a magnum of champagne. A leathersmith in Indio carved two vents in the sides and installed a mesh that permitted air to circulate. The leathersmith lengthened the loop so Hoby could carry the case over his shoulder. He lined the interior with soft felt. The case was made of black leather and was shaped like a projectile. Tulio thought it looked sinister. He knew what it was for, but he didn't let Hoby know that he had seen the creature. Why would Hoby want to carry the creature around with him? Why would he conceal it in a funny black bag?

He hoped Hoby hadn't gotten involved in witchcraft.

Hoby did not intend to fly to any of the locations; Otis would never pass undetected through the X-ray security machines. He told Lamar he preferred to drive everywhere in his old Buick. Lamar told him if the car gave out he could borrow one from the company pool. Lamar didn't care whether he drove; as long as he obtained results, he could walk if he wanted to. Clearly the fellow was no ordinary mortal. Maybe he ate peyote, maybe he indulged in secret rites, maybe his hands had been blessed by a monk destined for canonization. Lamar didn't know and he didn't care. Hoby did the job.

The morning before he left to travel upstate, Hoby and Lamar had a final interview in the Riverside office. Hoby's costume for the occasion differed from what he had worn three days earlier in San Bernardino: cotton slacks, a blue shirt stitched along the shoulders with floral designs, and Dingo boots. Over the shirt he wore a pinstriped vest; around his neck, knotted loosely, a red bandana. Strapped to his hips was a wide belt supporting a pair of empty holsters crafted of dark, shiny leather; Hoby had oiled them carefully.

"Why . . . them?" Lamar asked.

Hoby shrugged. "I think it's more powerful than carrying a gun. It's symbolic. It gives me the feeling that I'm packing a real weapon."

Lamar nodded agreeably.

"By wearing them, I'll alert all skeptical outlet managers that I'm not to be taken lightly. They can have their little laugh, but when I walk into their place I want them to know that I mean business. Plus, when my hands get tired from all the squeezing, I'll have a place to tuck them away."

"How about a hat to go with the rest of the outfit? Some spurs? A pair of chaps maybe?"

"No, sir. I don't wear hats. Not even in the desert. That other stuff I regard as so much costume frippery. I'm not a real cowboy, Mr. Whammers. I don't even know how to ride a horse."

Lamar stared at him a long time through a scrim of Canary Island cigar smoke. "You know what?" he said finally.

"No, sir. What?"

"I think I got a name for you."

"What's that?"

"I think I'm gonna call you the Ptomaine Kid."

12

The trip was a smash. From La Jolla to Petaluma, from Lake Tahoe to Calexico, Hoby Tibbs cut a triumphant swath. His fingers crackled. His touch was redemptive. By a stroke of incredible good fortune he had been blessed with the power to heal. Overnight, he took on a new look. He walked with a new step. He stared people straight in the eye when he spoke with them. His tongue didn't falter. He didn't stutter or equivocate. With each new day, with each new triumph, he became more confident and self-assured.

He entered a new town with little fanfare. He called the outlet and asked the manager what time he should show up the next morning. Nearly all the managers were incredulous at first. The appearance of this curious man, sporting a vest and a bandana, a pair of holsters strapped to his waist, provoked a flurry of smirks and titters. A few managers were downright insulting, regarding Hoby's appearance as some kind of publicity stunt dreamed up by L. G. Whammers. But when Hoby worked his magic, they stopped scoffing. They became hushed and respectful. They became believers. A memo from Whammers, circulated to all branch managers, may have helped: "I want this man treated with the same respect that you would accord to any hero whose exploits had saved your ass from the poorhouse."

Finished with his laborious kneading, usually at a late hour, Hoby stumbled back to his motel. There in a dingy room he poured himself a tall glass of Old Crow and propped up his feet. Otis was out of the case by then, sitting on the dresser. Although he never chirped or nodded, Hoby was sure he understood. Night after night, in towns like Santa Barbara, Bakersfield, Fresno, and Santa Cruz, he told Otis about his dream of someday owning his own hamburger stand and his affection for the Widow Rodriguez. In seedy hotels up and down the San Joaquin Valley, in grubby chalets high up in the Sierras, in crackerjack motels along the lower Colorado River, he waxed rhapsodic about the widow, describing her face and figure in glowing language. Up to now Hoby had been content to worship her from afar, but that was about to change. "Once I finish this trip and get my name up in lights, the lady will take notice," he burbled one night in a hotel room in downtown Stockton. "You hear that, Otis? Sooner or later everybody's gonna have to reckon with the likes of the Ptomaine Kid."

One drink followed another, decanted from the neck of the bottle, spilling over fresh ice cubes, a dark, tawny liquid in which Hoby, looking down into the glass, could see reflected his own smooth, appealing features.

"It's not a fancy place I'm wanting, Otis. On Indio Boulevard, right across from the Southern Pacific tracks. Location is important. That and the product. Can't forget the product. But, shit, that's in the bag. I'll have customers driving all the way from Rancho Mirage and Palm Springs. Maybe not that many, but enough to make it interesting. The slack'll be taken up by S.P. workers, Indio merchants, and truckers. Lots of trucks pass along that route because of the diesel stations outside town. Indio's a major distribution point for wholesale groceries and produce. Vegetables grown in the Imperial Valley first come to Indio before being shipped outside the state. So there's a variety of customers I can count on. Also braceros. You'd be surprised, Otis, how many Mexican fruit pickers like to sink their chops into a hamburger. I'll have a special burger for them. A slice of avocado, topped with a tangy salsa, a dish of pinto beans on the side.

"I got plans for a simple place, Otis. A counter with maybe a half-dozen stools. Maybe a half-dozen tables, four to a table. Maximum thirty-six customers, forty at the most. I can handle that many from the cooking end. Two waitresses . . . solid, steady gals with a sense of humor. One on the counter and one on the floor. I'll need an assistant to prepare the buns and garnish. Also to fix the toast and fry the bacon in the morning. A young kid who wants to learn the business. Then a combo busboy-dishwasher. I'll install one of those Wypo automatic dishwashers that one person can operate with no trouble."

Otis peered into the emptiness somewhere on the other side of the motel wall, his luminous eyes steady and transfixed. If he could only talk, Hoby thought.

"I got my work area all planned out. I been thinking about it a lot. A stainless steel counter in the center where I can lay out the buns and assemble the garnish. To the left, I'll set the grill. To my right the stove, where I'll deep-fry my onions and spuds and cook up my eggs. Did I tell you about my new hamburger? Hoby's Trucker Special. A fat, juicy patty served open-faced with a poached egg on top, flavored with a special salsa Tulio's mother will make for me. Great Jesus. Just the thought of it makes me smack my lips.

"A few posters on the walls, a few pictures. No nudie stuff. I'd like to serve beer, 'cause beer tastes good with hamburger. On the counter and the lower sections of the wall I'll have lots of white formica. It'll give the place a clean, sparkly look. Maybe a planter running along one wall, festooned with growing green things. I'd like a big bulletin board for postcards. I like postcards. I'll encourage my customers to send them to me. It's fun to look at them and think of other places.

"In the back storage room I'll keep a cot. Sometimes I'll want to spend the night to make sure everything's all right. I'll have the joint so well organized in a few weeks that it'll practically run itself. Got to devise an efficient schedule and stick to it. Be there at five in the morning sharp, ready to serve breakfast at six. Plenty of newspapers and good magazines on hand. Get to know everybody by their first name. Be friendly, cheerful, courteous. Shit, I can't miss. I speak a little Spanish, Otis, which'll please the Mexican clientele. Above all, good food. Stuff that'll send 'em out the door ready to tear up the world. For lunch a variety of soups plus a Fabulous Burger Hit Parade: Mexican burgers, Hawaiian burgers, Texas burgers, Dainty Lady burgers. Eggs and bacon and sausage anytime. Tuna fish and egg salad for variety, especially in summer when the thermometer cranks up. Shut down at four. Clean up for an hour. Go home, suck back on a bomber or a glass of Old Crow. Long day. Hard work. Eeee-haw!"

Otis sat motionless on the dresser, his warm yellow eyes fixed on no certain object. A profound, haunting, deep-set gaze that seemed to extend out beyond the street, beyond the tangle of cloverleaf off-and-on ramps at the edge of town, all the way to the dark mountains in the distance. "Best of all, big guy," Hoby said, getting to his feet, "best of all'll be the name over the door. HOBY'S. Or maybe HOBY'S BEST BURGERS. Naw, I like the first. Just the name. It's simpler, to the point. HOBY'S . . . HOBY'S."

He reeled against the dresser, rocking it against the wall, snatching up the creature before he teetered off the edge and hugging him to his chest. Otis didn't blink or cheep or groan. Cradling the creature, Hoby staggered to the bed and drew down the covers. Pulling off his boots, still wearing his pants and holsters, he stuck both legs under the sheets. He propped Otis on the pillow next to him, where he could reach out and stroke his downy fur. The eyes never bothered him. Not even in the dead of night when he woke up and saw them hovering in the dark like a pair of enameled wafers did the sight of them ever make him feel uneasy or apprehensive.

"G'night," he whispered, running his fingers over the soft, warm head.

13

Hoby returned to Indio after seventeen days on the road to find himself a celebrity. A reporter in Needles got wind of what he was doing and interviewed the local WhammyBurger manager after Hoby had left town. The manager told the reporter to call Ralph Manning at the Riverside office. Ralph was noncommittal over the phone. The reporter knew he was on to something. From a dishwasher in the Needles outlet he found out Hoby's name and the fact that he lived in Indio. He called a colleague at the *Indio Daily News* and asked him if he could dig up anything. The colleague found out that one Hobart Tibbs was going around California curing an outbreak of bad hamburger meat. The "phantom healer" was how both reporters described Hoby's activities in their respective newspapers. The evening before Hoby returned to Indio, a local TV station had picked up the story and run a feature on it in a section of its 6:00 news known as "Desert Personalities." Randolph Tibbs watched that newscast regularly. So did Tulio Sanchez.

"What's this about you got some strange power?" Tulio asked casually the evening Hoby returned. They were sitting in front of the duplex, smoking a number and drinking beer. The sun had dropped behind the San Jacinto Mountain; a creamy orange light filled the air inside the date orchard. Bats darted between the palms.

"Where did you hear that?"

"Last night on the news. Your old man heard it, too. He called me a couple of times."

"What did he want?"

"Just to say hello. He sounded kind of drunk. He said he thought you were getting to be some kind of big shot."

"I wonder how that story got around."

"On the news last night they said it first appeared in a paper in Needles."

Hoby sucked on the joint and took a swig of beer. Tulio didn't tell him that he had seen the creature and that the creature had given him the willies. One evening while Hoby was away, he had driven down to Mecca, on the north shore of the Salton Sea, to talk with his grandfather. He told him about the creature, describing it carefully, especially the eyes. The old man made a clicking noise with his dentures and rolled a cigarette. He said he had heard of the creature but never seen it. When he was a boy he knew of some people in the Sierra Madres of Sonora who had seen one.

"Is it a bird?" Tulio wondered.

"Not exactly," the old man replied. "Nobody really knows what it is. It seems to be from this world. It looks like a bird, but it isn't. Brujos are able to summon them when they need help. They are powerful at the same time they are gentle and docile. It appears usually at the behest of an urgent summons, in times of great crisis and trial."

"But how could a gringo make one appear?"

The grandfather shrugged and sipped on the tip of his hand-rolled cigarette. "I don't know the answer to that," he said.

"Would you like to see it?"

"Well, yes, of course. But no. It's not my place to see it unless it chooses for me to do so. You saw it by accident, when you weren't looking for it, and there's something correct about that. But for you to arrange for me to see it would be wrong. If the creature wants me to see it, it will happen."

Hoby took a sip from the bottle of Carta Blanca and handed the joint back to Tulio. "I like it here," he sighed. "I been all over California, and there's no place like this place. I don't want the widow to sell it out from under us."

"I heard the rumor again at Patencio's."

"Why would she do that?"

"To make money."

"She already has plenty of money."

"Maybe she wants more."

"But that's not right!" Hoby exclaimed. "This place is paradise. It may be an investment to her, but to us it's the Garden of Eden!"

"Why don't you ask her yourself?"

"What? Call her up and chew the fat? 'Allo, senora, you don't know me, my name ees 'oby Teebs . . .'"

"You can speak to her tonight."

"Tonight?"

"Sure. She's singing here in town tonight at the Shalimar Auditorium. Tonight at eight she's giving a recital."

"Why didn't you tell me!"

"Shoot, Hoby, how am I to know who you got a hard-on for? You're such a closed-mouth guy."

Hoby bolted out of the chair and ran into his house and started pulling off his clothes. He was down to his boxer shorts and heading for the shower when the phone rang. "Hello!" he barked.

"Hoby, my boy!" It was L.G. Whammers. "Have you heard the news?"

"What news, Mr. Whammers? I been in the car all day, driving from China Lake."

"Well, my boy, you're on your way to being famous. This evening you were featured on the Channel 7 news from Los Angeles. Seems that people are becoming more aware of your exploits."

"How come that's so, Mr. Whammers? I thought you wanted it kept a secret."

"I did, Hoby, but no more, no more. The account of your exploits has raised such a fuss that the FDA is going to open a full-scale investigation into the matter of tainted hamburger. Normally, I'd be worried any time the feds start poking their noses into our business. But this time I feel certain the results will go our way. Such an investigation is bound to drive up the price of hamburger so we can tack a little something onto our own burgers with full government justification. Ah, Hoby, if you were here right now I'd kiss you on the cheek! I've called a press conference here at the Riverside office for tomorrow afternoon. You will be the featured attraction."

"Mr. Whammers, I been on the road for seventeen days and I'm tired. I don't want to drive up to Riverside tomorrow."

"You don't have to, my boy. I'm sending an aircraft down to pick you up. Be at the Bermuda Dunes airport at 1:00 p.m. tomorrow. You'll be met by Captain Wilcox, pilot of our company's Commander Jetprop."

"I'm not sure this is a good idea, Mr. Whammers . . ."

"It's too late for that, Hoby. If you didn't want to become famous, then you shouldn't have shown anybody what you can do with your hands. The track has been greased. You're on your way to the Big Time."

The phone wouldn't stop ringing. As he stepped out of the shower,

Deeter Jester called to welcome him back and offer congratulations. "Looks like we won't be seeing you much any more at the old PD Burger Plant, hot shot. We're gonna miss you."

Then, as he was knotting a tie around the collar of a white shirt, his father called. "You done it now, son," he growled, his scarred tongue slurping over the words. "I reckon you can open up that hamburger stand pretty damn well where you want to now."

"Not for awhile yet, Dad."

"How so?"

"There's lots of sick hamburger out there that needs tending to."

"Just make sure they pay you what you're worth, son."

"They're being very generous, Dad . . ."

"How much are they paying you?"

"A hundred dollars a day, plus expenses," he lied.

"Shit, that's not enough to fill the belly of a cockroach! What do they think things cost today? You ask them for more."

"Will do, Pop."

"Lousy skinflint bastards. They got theirs. What the hell have they got against someone else getting his own?"

Hoby pinched the phone between his neck and shoulder and tried to button his collar.

"I don't know what your secret is, son, but whatever it is get a patent on it and you'll make a million. But get a patent on it before some rotten son of a bitch steals it from you."

"It's not really a secret, Dad. I don't know exactly what it is."

"Bottle it, cap it, box it, tube it, label it," Randolph advised.

Unable to button his collar even with two hands, Hoby gave up and told his father about the press conference the next afternoon.

"Son, I'm so proud of you I'm about to bust. Just make sure they spell the name right. That's Tibbs, with two b's."

"Sure, Pop. You betcha."

14

Maybe he should wear a disguise. If he was becoming that well-known, maybe he should conceal his features so he wouldn't be hounded in the auditorium by people seeking his autograph. He was ambivalent about his newly acquired status. He appreciated the money and attention, but he was fearful that too much notoriety would complicate the desire to own his own hamburger place. That's all he really wanted. He wanted the money to secure the place and a little of the fame to ensure a steady flow of customers. He also wanted to remain in the orchard with Tulio and Fiona. If the widow recognized who he was, she might be less inclined to sell the place.

A disguise seemed like a good idea. From behind it Hoby could listen to the widow perform. He had scissors in hand and was creeping toward the window when he caught himself. Otis sat motionless on the flat top of the air conditioner that fit neatly below the window. He was facing the glass, gazing out through a gap in the foliage at the Little San Bernardino Mountains. The sun had disappeared, and the ravines and gullies etching the features of the distant mountains were swathed in deep purple shadows. Hoby needed a disguise—a mustache and sideburns. A few snips from Otis's downy pelt would work just fine. But he couldn't bring himself to apply the scissors.

Instead he snipped a few swatches from the mouton collar of his winter jacket. He dabbed a drop or two of Fiona's clear fingernail polish to his jaw and upper lip and affixed the swatches to the appropriate places. Highlighted by a bold, reddish tint, the mouton contrasted strikingly with his dark, curly hair.

"Hoby, you look so handsome!" cried Fiona. She was sitting in the same lawn chair as Tulio, cuddled against him. Tulio took one look at him and began to laugh.

"You look like Rhett Butler," said Fiona.

"You look like Rhett Butler's dog," Tulio guffawed.

"Tulio, watch your mouth!"

"What's his dog look like?" said Hoby. "I've never seen his dog."

Tulio snorted. Fiona tried to jam her elbow into his mouth, but Tulio ducked. The momentum tipped the lawn chair over, and they sprawled into the grass.

"What time is it?" Hoby demanded.

"Quarter to eight."

"I better git."

"What's your hurry, man? The auditorium is five minutes away."

"I want to get a good seat."

He high-stepped down the sandy lane toward Oasis Street, wearing a pin-striped Haspel seersucker suit, the sleeves drooping to his thumbs. Moving at a rapid clip, he emerged from the orchard's shady depths, his heels tapping across the sidewalk. A dry breeze ruffled his fluffy hair. The marijuana smoke in his combustible brain magnified the urgency of his mission. He was on his way to hear the Widow Rodriguez, to exult in the grandeur of her voice. Afterward, he intended to confront her with the fact of his ardent affection. The pitch he would make on his behalf would be couched in such compelling rhetoric that she would be instantly sympathetic. She would grasp his hand and squeeze it. She would look deep into his eyes. She would wet her lips with her tongue and invite him back to her house for a nightcap . . .

He arrived late despite the speed with which he motored through the warm desert air, working up a light sweat that caused his newly acquired facial hair to itch in spots. Shalimar Auditorium was located on the site of the Indio Date Harvest Festival Grounds. A modest arena, with a seating capacity of six hundred, its walls were decorated with colorful murals commemorating the growth of the date industry in the Coachella Valley, starting with the importation of the first date palms from North Africa in the 1890s. The ticket cost five bucks. Hoby got one of the last available and squeezed into a seat on the far left side of the orchestra section.

The theater was packed with Indio's finest—blacks, Chicanos, and Anglos. Amanda Rodriguez occupied a special niche in the townspeople's affections. She had been born in Indio, gone to school there. Her grandparents were humble grape pickers from Michoacan. At age eighteen, Amanda won a scholarship to study voice at UCLA. While in college she met another student from the area, a tall, long-legged, fair-complected fellow named Peter Rodriguez. The Rodriguez family had been in the Coachella Valley since the 1880s and over the generations had acquired extensive holdings along the northern and western shores of the Salton Sea—land originally deemed worthless by most Anglos but that had been shrewdly appraised for its potential value by Joachim Rodriguez, Peter's grandfather and the patriarch of the family. Peter and Amanda had married when he was twenty-four and she was twenty-two. His parents, though of Mexican descent, were scandalized at the prospect of their son marrying the granddaughter of a wetback. But Amanda—a woman of intelligence and charm as well as ambition—captivated her in-laws and worked diligently to make both her marriage and her singing career a success.

By all accounts the marriage had been just that. Although childless and frequently separated for long periods, the couple appeared devoted to one another. There were trysts on both sides, but they had been discreetly maintained, without the least whiff of scandal. Peter's untimely death raised a question or two, but the good luck that followed him throughout his life carried on after his death. Returning home one night from Brawley in the Imperial Valley, driving on Highway 86—a narrow, perilous road that follows the western shore of the Salton Sea—his car struck a bridge and caromed off the road, rolling over a half-dozen times along a sandy wash. Peter's neck snapped like a bean pod, killing him instantly. Witnesses in Westmoreland, who had seen Peter in a tavern an hour before the accident, swore that he had been with a woman, but she was never located or identified.

Amanda was in Caracas at the time, appearing in an opera by Manuel de Falla. At the funeral she wore a simple black dress highlighted by a white rose pinned to her shoulder. Her appearance, according to everyone who was there, had been tragic and aggrieved; clearly she was shattered by the blow. That had been four years ago. Since then Amanda had pulled the pieces together. Within a short time, she developed into a skillful manager of her late husband's properties, which included the orchard currently tenanted by Tulio Sanchez and Hobart Tibbs. She resumed her singing career, appearing with the San Diego and Santa Fe operas. Tonight's recital in Shalimar Auditorium marked the first time she had appeared in Indio professionally in nearly ten years. The occasion was a fund-raiser for a hospital for crippled children to be constructed in the city at a future date.

She swept onstage, accompanied by her pianist. She wore a linen dress, exquisitely tailored with simple lines, a rich, cerulean blue. A string of lustrous pearls hung from her neck. Her thick black hair was swept back from her face into a luxurious pile. A pair of tortoise-shell combs trimmed with gold pegged the pile into place. The applause that greeted her was warm and enthusiastic. The pianist took his place. The applause faded. The piano started up with a rumble, followed a moment later by the throaty warble of her voice.

She sang a medley of Spanish folksongs based on gypsy ballads collected by Federico Garcia Lorca. Her knock-out presence, her impeccable phrasing, her statuesque figure . . . a shiver rippled up Hoby's spine.

After the recital there was a reception. Before Hoby could get in he had to fork over fifty dollars—part of the fund-raising campaign. Fortunately, he had plenty of cash. The reception was in an anteroom. Hoby pulled at his tie and sauntered through the door.

Unbeknownst to him, the heat had caused his mouton facial hair to shift on his jaw. His left sideburn had detached itself from his scalp and curled up on his cheek like a loose bandaid.

Hoby took his place at the end of the receiving line, cradling a glass of tequila punch. The mayor of Indio, whom he knew slightly, stood next to the widow in the receiving line. Hoby's mustache began to itch. He scratched it and looked aghast when a few flakes came off in his hand. Frantically, as the line moved up, people talking and joking, he clawed at his cheeks and lip, tearing off clots of sticky, reddish-brown hair.

He was nearing the head of the line. His heart pounded in a frenzy. He dug at his cheekbones, tearing loose more patches of hair. He thought he'd gotten most of the sideburns when the person in front of him pushed on, and he found himself face to face with Amanda Rodriguez.

Up close, her features were magnified. Her nostrils quivered, her eyes shone with a rich luster. She was taller than he expected, an inch or two taller than him. Her plum-red lips were enticingly full. Her hand closed around his. Hoby's toes turned to ice.

"You . . . you were magnificent . . . *señora*," he managed to say.

"That's very kind of you, Mr. . . . Mr. . . . ?"

"Tibbs, ma'am. Hobart Tibbs . . ."

His hand encased in the soft flesh of hers hummed like a generator.

" . . . although you might recognize me by my new name . . . the Ptomaine Kid."

The widow looked puzzled. But the mayor, a short, stout man named Alphonse Ruiz, grabbed his hand and pumped it up and down.

"Of course, Mr. Kid, we heard about your exploits on television! How do you do, Mr. Kid! It is a pleasure to make your acquaintance."

Her eyes still fixed on Hoby, the widow whispered to the mayor, *"Quién es?"*

"El es el curandero de hamburguesas cuyo apodo es, chico de tomaina."

Her face brightened. Her teeth flashed a gracious smile. "It is indeed nice to know you. We are all very proud of the work you are doing. Without healthy hamburger, I don't know what would become of this country. Your cause is just and noble."

Hoby was flabbergasted. "You think so?"

"Indeed, Mr. Tibbs. You are one of the heroes of the contemporary world. You are saving the food for the people. Keep up the magnificent work."

Hoby found himself being passed on down the line in a daze. He shook hands with the mayor again. He shook hands with the mayor's wife and two teenage daughters. Still cupping the glass of punch, he plodded around the room gripping other hands, nodding and grinning.

People shied away or grinned nervously. Maybe it was the patches of mouton facial hair, glistening like a poison ivy rash. Maybe it was the glint in his eye: frigid, glassy, cockamamied. A security guard gave him the once-over. Hoby was delirious. He skated over to the punch bowl and downed three quick glasses. The tequila jerked him upright. He downed two more glasses. Then he remembered that he hadn't mentioned the date orchard to the widow. He popped his forehead with his palm and looked around. The widow was gone. The room was full of people, but the one who meant more to him than all the others was no longer there.

15

Possibly, just possibly, he hadn't made too big a fool of himself. Despite the facial hair, she seemed impressed with him. Like Alphonse Ruiz, she had heard of him. His name, his identity, meant something to her. She had complimented him on being who he was. How many people could say that about themselves? Hoby Tibbs, the Ptomaine Kid. It was a name to be proud of. It was a title a fellow could keep.

From the window of the two-engine Commander Jet-Prop, he looked down 4,000 feet to the sandy floor of the San Gorgonio Pass. He was hopelessly in love, an oafish, adolescent love. Between the two of them, for a moment there had been the kind of communication that bridged the gap between their respective backgrounds. A little piece of his heart had fused itself around her finger. In the future, all she had to do was crook the finger, and the rest of his heart would unravel like a spool of yarn.

Thirty minutes later the aircraft touched down at the Riverside airport, and Hobby was shuttled into a waiting Mercedes for the trip downtown to the WhammyBurger office. He arrived in costume: boots, levis, denim shirt, checkered vest, silk bandana, shiny black holsters with a hand-tooled cartridge belt strapped around his waist. The reporters loved it. Still cameras popped and flashed. TV cameras whirred, shooting yards of footage for the evening news. Newspapers and TV stations from San Diego, Los Angeles, San Bernardino, and the Coachella Valley were there. At first Hoby tried to fade back into the shadows. But after fielding a few questions, his awkwardness disappeared. I can do this, he decided. I can give them what they want.

The conference was held in Lamar's office. The conference table had been pulled out to the center of the room. Hoby sat at one end, facing a battery of microphones, a dozen reporters bunched around him. Over their shoulders and between their elbows poked the lenses of video cameras like fish eyes from another depth . . . dull, lifeless, unblinking.

"How come you don't carry guns in those holsters?" asked a woman from the *San Diego Union.*

"'Cause my guns are attached to my wrists," Hoby replied, giving his fingers a shake.

"Can you tell us when you first knew you had this power?"

"I woke up one morning, and it was there."

"Was it accompanied by any special feeling?"

"One of great relief, actually. I felt as if I'd been waiting all my life for this moment."

"When you put your hands into the hamburger, is there any special sensation that you experience?"

"Yes, I would say there is. A heightened sense of expectation. A tingling thrill of danger and the unknown. Similar, I suspect, to sticking your hands into a shark's mouth."

"Shark's mouth . . . whooo!" The reporters scribbled furiously, the cameras clicked and whirred. Lightbulbs popped and flashed. Hoby leaned back in the chair and winked at L. G. Whammers.

"Mr. Tibbs, do you think you can heal all the bad hamburger in America?" asked a sallow-faced young man from the *Los Angeles Times.*

"No, sir, I don't. It would be arrogant of me to assume so. First of all, I don't know how much hamburger in America is sick. If it's all sick, then we're in big trouble, 'cause I don't think anybody—no matter how great their gift—has the energy and imagination to cure that much. Second, for the moment I'm working for Mr. Whammers. My job is to take care of the tainted hamburger that surfaces in his establishments. Right now, that's my main job."

"Do you look upon yourself as some kind of savior?" This, breathlessly, from a reporter at the *Desert Sun.*

"No, ma'am," said Hoby, looking humble. "I look upon myself as an ordinary man with a knack for doing an extraordinary job."

"If that's all the questions, ladies and gentlemen, I'd like to say a few words."

Lamar sat behind his desk, puffing the inevitable Canary Island cigarillo. He stood up and took a seat next to Hoby at the conference table. He was smartly dressed in a lightweight summer suit with dark stitching along the collar and around the pockets. A silk handkerchief drooped from the breast pocket. A lapis lazuli ring banded his left pinky.

"It's no secret that an epidemic of ptomaine poisoning has struck several hamburger franchises in California and the Southwest," he began somberly. "Next week the Food and Drug Administration will launch a full-scale investigation into the causes. In the meantime, we of the WhammyBurger organization intend to launch our own response to this terrible malady. For the past thirty minutes, you ladies and gentlemen of the press have been interviewing one of the most remarkable men in America. Hobart Tibbs, chef extraordinaire at the Palm Desert WhammyBurger, has recently acquired—by what process I do not know—a phenomenal aptitude for curing bad hamburger meat. He has been kind enough to offer his services to our organization. Beginning next week, Hoby will embark on a personal crusade that will take him through Arizona, New Mexico, and west Texas. Alone, and armed only with the power of his extraordinary hands, he intends to do battle with this frightful scourge.

"In the meantime, in all those outlets where poisoning has been reported, I have ordered a moratorium on hamburger cooking until Hoby Tibbs declares the meat in those places to be free of pestilence. For twenty years, the WhammyBurger organization has tried to bring the best in fast foods to the American public. And while we firmly believe that our hamburger is finer than that of our competitors, we are prepared to go one better in these difficult times by offering an additional service no other franchise can offer. I'm talking about Mr. Hoby Tibbs. Yes, ladies and gentlemen, sitting right here in this office is the latest secret weapon of the WhammyBurger organization: the man who, with the power of his fingers alone, can heal bad hamburger meat. As of next Monday, he will be out on the road doing just that."

Lamar's hushed, dramatic voice made Hoby squirm. But for $425 a day—the terms of his new contract, negotiated after the successful California trip—he could squirm all he wanted.

"My associate, Ralph Manning, will be in daily contact with Hoby and will alert the media and the public immediately after the ptomaine microbes have been successfully removed from each of our afflicted outlets. Ralph is a seventeen-year veteran of our staff, a recognized industry expert, and one of my most trusted associates."

Hoby perked up his ears. Lamar hadn't told him Ralph would be involved, even as a liaison. Lamar knew better than that. Hoby didn't like Ralph. Ralph was a fink, a punk, who put his loyalty to the organization ahead of everything else. Hoby didn't trust him. He didn't like the way Ralph's lip curled when he was confronted by something he didn't understand or couldn't control. Ralph didn't know anything about cooking or eating hamburgers. He just knew how to sell them. He was a marketing guy, a computer printout geek, a numbers cruncher. All Ralph cared about was volume.

The conference broke up. Hoby posed for a few stills with Ralph and Lamar—grudgingly, without a smile. The reporters wanted an action shot, Hoby in a gunfighter's crouch, hands sweeping up from his holsters. Hoby refused. Ralph told him it would be great publicity. Hoby snarled. Lamar pulled him aside and offered him a cigarillo. No use antagonizing his star performer, the man who would not only fix his hamburger but fix the name of the WhammyBurger franchise in the national eye.

"Relax," he told Hoby. "Calm down. Save your strength."

You'll be needing it, he added silently under his breath.

16

"Grandfather, I saw the creature again."

The old man had only one eye. He shifted his gaze down from the top of the tall Washingtonian palm that rattled over his modest shack on the shore of the Salton Sea and settled it on his grandson's face.

"Last night my friend went out to hear the Widow Rodriguez sing, and when he was gone I snuck into his house. The creature was in the bedroom, sitting on the air conditioner, staring out the window. It scared me a little. I stood in the door and watched it. I wanted to get closer to it, maybe even touch it, but I couldn't. I got the feeling that if I touched it something really bad would happen to me."

"It's not something to trifle with," the old man agreed, flicking the ash off the crinkly tip of a hand-rolled cigarette.

"I'm sure that's where my friend gets his power to cure sick hamburger meat. In the last three weeks he's been everywhere in California healing the bad stuff with the touch of his fingers. He didn't have that power before he found the creature. I'm in his house a lot, and the first time I saw the creature was three weeks ago before he left on his trip."

"He's wasting his time," the old man growled.

"What do you mean?"

"That's not what the creature is for. Your friend doesn't understand its true power."

Tulio lit a cigarette and blew smoke into the air. "So what do you think he should do with it?"

"Nothing. It's not his to do anything with. The creature is a gift. A blessing. Its power is such that if it chooses, it can give anybody anything. So it helps make a few hamburgers edible again. So what? There is so much poison in the world that cleaning up a few hamburgers won't make any difference. If the hamburger is meant to be poisoned, then let's forget about it and never eat another one again."

"But my friend can't live without hamburger. It's his whole life."

The old man chuckled, squinting with one eye across the road, over the beet field, at the shimmering expanse of the Salton Sea, a body of dead, gluey water, formed by the rampaging waters of the Colorado River in the early 1900s. "It's a stupid reason. The creature did not appear merely to enable your friend to do that. He can live without hamburger, good or bad. I don't pretend to know why the creature singled him out. Probably he happened upon it by accident. The kind of power the creature has should not be wasted on trifles. It should not be wasted on curing something already hopelessly tainted."

"I don't understand."

"I'm not sure I do either. I'm only guessing. Every day I sit on the porch of this house and stare up at the palms and out at the water and try and puzzle out what it is that makes the world the way it is. I used to believe it was God who made it happen. Now I'm not so sure. It still is God, I suppose, only so many other things get in the way."

Tulio sucked deeply on the cigarette, smiling inwardly as the smoke coiled into the sky.

"I will tell you this . . ." The old man fastened his one good eye onto his grandson's face. "If the creature appeared to me, I would take it into the mountains, far up to a special place. I wouldn't eat anything for a few days and would drink only a little water. I would pray and pray. And then I would listen for a response. I would try and learn what it was the creature had singled me out for. After I had learned, I would come back here and gather up what I needed and go up into the mountains and never come back."

17

It began in Yuma, a few blocks from the old territorial prison. There was a WhammyBurger there and one out on the east edge of town in a shopping mall. Hoby took care of that one first; then in the afternoon, he moved to the one in town, within rock-lobbing distance of the Colorado River. It was a new place with a slick plastic front, made to look like an adobe mission, with a fake bell tower peaking off the roof. The tower actually chimed on the hour, a melodious ripple of computer-generated bells that could be heard over the snort of traffic.

Hoby arrived at 1:30, in costume, carrying the black leather trophy bag. It was hot, the first week in June. The sun blazed down. The front-door handle singed his fingers. Inside it was cool. On the wall were several sepia-tinted photo reproductions of life in old Yuma: Mohave Indians wearing turbans, the Colorado River at full flood, a desperado dangling from a noose over the heads of two grinning urchins.

The proprietors, Mae and Idaman Hargett, were awestruck by Hoby's presence. Word had gone out from the Riverside headquarters to all afflicted outlets that the Ptomaine Kid would be riding into their towns to do battle with the pernicious microbes. The Hargetts, like many other operators, had put their life savings into the purchase of the franchise license. The sight of this modest man with fair skin, curly hair, and a brace of empty holsters sliding through the door filled them with both elation and anxiety.

Mae Hargett had a frosty Coke waiting for the Kid. Idaman found the grip of the healer's hand curiously noncommittal. Idaman may have resembled a yokel with his thatch of yeast-colored hair and pronounced Adam's apple, but he was shrewd enough to discern the wellsprings of iron and resilience lurking underneath the Kid's bland demeanor.

Two hours later, with the heat pouring down in molten sheets, Hoby squatted in an alley between a couple of buildings across the street from the Hargett establishment. Two work sessions a day made his hands and forearms ache, but before he returned to the hotel to plunge them into a sink full of warm tap water, he wanted to check something out. Despite his soft, pulpy figure that tended to a kind of creamy flabbiness, his bones and joints were flexible, possessing the kind of elasticity and suppleness that enabled him, like his father, to hunker down on his haunches for long periods of time. Hoby unzipped the top of the black leather bag to allow a little air to circulate. "Just for a bit, Otis," he murmured. "Then we'll get back into the air conditioning."

Ten minutes after Hoby had settled himself in a deep shadow in the alley, a car pulled up and Ralph Manning stepped out. Hoby shifted the toothpick to the other side of his mouth. Interesting, he thought. Ostensibly, Ralph was there to check the results of his handiwork. Ostensibly, too, he was there to telephone the results back to the Riverside office. Hoby could easily make the call himself, but Lamar had made it clear that the follow-up to every job Hoby performed would be Ralph Manning's responsibility.

Hoby was puzzled. He rolled the toothpick around in his mouth. Something peculiar was going on that he couldn't account for. Was Ralph stalking him for a reason other than merely verifying the results of his labor?

Later, after a nap and a shower in his motel, he went back into the streets without the trophy bag and holsters. It was past six; the heat was still fierce. The buildings downtown seemed to shimmer and warp into a variety of mystifying shapes.

Hoby was thirsty. He'd eaten supper, now he was ready for some liquid refreshment. There was a bar on the same street as the WhammyBurger franchise—Little Nell's—with pink lights beaming in the window.

People were playing pool or perched up at the bar, staring into an aquarium filled with flat, ugly fish. The jukebox was silent, the conversation desultory; despite the best efforts of the two air conditioning units, the heat from the streets crept inside and settled on every surface like a sticky wax. The bartender, Little Nell, a stout, florid woman, laid her cheek against the aquarium glass and rolled her eyes enviously at the creatures immersed within. Hoby drank two quick beers, then sipped a third.

An ad for a local beer, mounted on the wall over the aquarium, caught Hoby's eye. It was an illuminated drawing of a bare-breasted woman suckling a malnourished beaver. The beaver's pelt was pocked and frowsy. The woman knelt beside a creek, a beaver mound and dam visible over her right shoulder. The expression on the beaver's face, with the nipple wedged under its protuberant teeth, was blissful and reposed. The caption read, "Bill Sublette's Widow Makes Amends for Her Trapper Husband's Excesses." The brewery was located in New Mexico—Popé Cerveza. Hoby ordered a bottle. It tasted like the milk from a lactating cow. He belched and ordered a shot of Old Crow to cut the suds.

18

In Phoenix, Ralph arrived a few minutes after Hoby finished working over the meat in each of the six area franchises. Standing across the street or sitting in the Buick, Hoby observed Ralph's tall figure, attaché case in hand, striding purposefully through the door. The way he walked annoyed Hoby. Ralph walked like a tractor, oblivious of everything in his path. Long churning strides, his wingtip shoes thumping against the soft pavement . . . clomp clomp clomp.

Hoby watched and smoldered.

Lamar wasn't much help when he called to complain. "Hoby . . . Hoby," he purred over the receiver,"that's Ralph's job. He's got to certify what you did, plus do the necessary paper work. I don't want to bother you with that stuff. I want you to be free to concentrate on the hamburger. Your job is to heal, Hoby. And from what I hear, you're doing an incredible job. I got a display board here in my office, an enlarged map of the Southwest, with red pins sticking in every place there's an afflicted franchise. Soon as Ralph calls and tells me the problem's been cleared up, I take out the red pin and replace it with a blue one. So far I've done that for eight places, Hoby, two in Yuma and six in Phoenix.

"Everyday we get calls from our competition, wondering when they can use your services. The ptomaine epidemic is killing them. Their sales are down 40 percent. Whereas every time we declare another WhammyBurger microbe-free, it's swamped with customers. You're doing an outstanding job, Hoby. Now just relax and let Ralph do his . . ."

Despite Lamar's reassuring tone, Hoby couldn't rid himself of a nagging suspicion. One day a television crew followed him around, but Hoby wouldn't let them into the outlet to film him curing the hamburger. When they complained, he told them that such proceedings were strictly off limits to anyone not officially connected to the WhammyBurger organization. "But a Mr. Ralph Manning from your executive office told us it was okay," one of the crewmen whined.

"I don't care what he told you. It's not okay."

Ralph was becoming a pest.

The next night in Scottsdale he followed Ralph to a fancy Mexican restaurant. From a secluded place at the bar, he observed him having dinner with two men, a couple of grunts of indiscernible ethnic origin wearing shimmery acrylic suits right off the J. C. Penney rack. After dinner they remained at the table talking for two hours. Ralph brought out papers and computer sheets from his briefcase and showed them to the others. After his eighth piña colada, Hoby slipped off the barstool. Maybe those guys were Ralph's in-laws, maybe they were from the IRS, maybe they were Mormons down from Salt Lake City. Hoby had no idea. High finance was like algebra to him. All he wanted was his own place and the license to cook the best hamburgers in the world.

19

The next afternoon in Ajo, a copper-mining town on the western edge of the Papago Indian Reservation, Hoby strode into the lone WhammyBurger outlet wearing his holsters and carrying the trophy bag.

"Thanks for coming. It's good to see you," the manager whispered in his ear as he guided Hoby into the kitchen out of sight of the customers. "We don't need you. We haven't had any trouble."

Hoby clicked his tongue against his teeth. The piña coladas the night before had turned his throat into a patch of sandpaper. He asked for a frosty Pepsi-Cola. "What makes this place different from the others?"

"We don't get our meat from the Riverside office," the manager replied. "Our meat comes from a supplier in Tucson. We're the only WhammyBurger in the state that enjoys this deal. Every other franchise is supplied by trucks that come out of Riverside."

"You've not had any trouble?"

"Not yet," the man said, rapping the side of his head with his knuckles. "I guess we been lucky. Sorry you came all this way for nothing. It was sure nice meeting you anyway. I saw you on TV the other day. You're getting to be real well-known in these parts."

Outside in the fiery street, Hoby was about to swing back into the Buick when a man limped out of the shadow of an empty storefront and laid his hand on the door handle. "You're the fella they refer to as the Ptomaine Kid, aintcha?"

"That's correct."

"Well, sir, I wonder if I could ask you a big favor. My name's Phelps. Harvey Phelps. I run the diner out south of town, next to the copper plant. I got a problem, a really big problem. See, most of my customers work in the plant. Indians and Chicanos, with appetites as big as a mountain. Well, sir, in the last few days my hamburger's gone bad on me. I don't know why, but when I fry up a patty it turns green and stinks something awful. Now these folks take their hamburger serious. At lunchtime they flock to my place and order a couple apiece. I don't know if you ever worked in a copper-smelting plant, Mister, but it's hard work, and you can really sweat up a big appetite. They're my main customers, and they're dead loyal to me, and I don't have any hamburger to feed them. So I wonder if you could help me out. I heard last night that you was coming to town, and I thought I could just ask you. I know you work exclusively for the WhammyBurger people, and I respect that. They make a fine hamburger, and I sure wouldn't have come up to you if I wasn't plain desperate. I'm on my last legs, Mister. If I don't do something about my sick hamburger, not only am I gonna lose my customers, I might lose my place. See, I'm mortgaged up to my ears to a bank in Tucson. Do you think you could help me out? I can't pay you much, maybe fifty dollars, but I sure would be grateful. So would my customers. They're tired of egg salad sandwiches. Chicken noodle soup don't cut it with them neither. These fellas need hamburger to get through the day."

Maybe it was the sun, flanging off the pavement, that made Hoby wince. That and the $425 he would forfeit for losing a day's work. But this man was in trouble. He looked worried. His chin was matted with stubble. His eyes rolled fitfully around his face.

"Sure . . . okay . . . where's your place?"

"Bless you, Mister, bless you!" Harvey Phelps whooped, hopping up and down on the soft pavement.

Hoby followed him through the streets of Ajo, past blocks of well-tended adobe bungalows, past a whitewashed church, to the diner, located close to the railroad tracks that curved out of the belly of the copper-smelting plant. Along the west side of the plant, stretching for a half mile, was a huge crust of earth, fifty feet high, part of the rim of a vast hole that over the years had been gouged and dozed out of the earth. A perimeter of slag and rubble that glinted in the bright sun with a garish, blue-green tincture. Hoby looped the trophy case around his wrist and followed Harvey Phelps across the street into the diner.

There was a gang of men inside, wearing greasy coveralls and work shirts. The midday shift, enjoying a late lunch, served by Phelps's wife and daughter, mainly soup from a tureen and chicken salad sandwiches. The decor was simple: a counter, eight tables, tasteful calendars on the walls, air conditioners at each window. The jukebox was honking, but not loud enough to drown out the complaints of the discontented workers. Phelps's wife and daughter worked frantically to serve them, ignoring the grumbles and nasty remarks, piling on extra helpings of french fries.

Phelps didn't introduce Hoby. He didn't say anything to his wife and daughter. He steered Hoby straight into the kitchen to the refrigerator. The meat was stored there in a pair of reinforced boxes. "Here it is," he said, pulling the boxes out and clunking them down on the counter. "Here's the godawful junk that's been causing me such misery."

"Hey, Harvey!" yelled a worker. "When can we stop eating this crap and sink our teeth into something worthwhile?"

"Yeah, Harvey. We're sick of iguana food. We want some meat."

The two women dashed for the coffeepots and began refilling everyone's cup. Harvey went out to the counter. Hoby could hear him explaining the problem in a supplicating voice. The workers hooted and razzed, then started in with insults. Harvey tried to banter with them, to deflect their anger by blaming the existence of bad hamburger on the ills of the world, but the workers were in no mood to be humored. They wanted their hamburger, and they wanted it now.

Hoby found a safe spot for the trophy bag and rolled up his sleeves. He dumped the contents of both boxes on the counter. The hamburger was in pitiful condition, globs of grainy red meat crawling with microbes.

An hour later he raised his weary hands over the mangled stack and shook the last sticky flecks from his fingers. The microbes had vanished. Hoby couldn't see them anymore; his hands no longer tingled, a definite indication that the poison had been removed. Harvey's wife tromped in twice, the first time to scold the stranger who had invaded her sanctuary, the second time to gape at the stranger's delicate white hands as they probed and flashed through the meat.

"Finished?" Phelps asked, running a hand nervously through his closely cropped hair.

Hoby nodded.

"How is it?"

"Should be okay."

"You want to test it with anything?"

"Don't need to. I can tell it's okay by looking at it."

Phelps rubbed a hand over the bristly stubble on his chin. "You can see the stuff in there?"

"That's right."

"Is this the fella that's been talked about on the television?" Mrs. Phelps wanted to know.

"The very one," Phelps said.

"What time's your next shift due in?" Hoby asked.

"Forty minutes!" snapped the daughter. "And Mister, if you think I'm gonna believe you cured that hamburger by the pressure of your fingers alone, you got a screw loose somewhere or you were born under a rock during an evil phase of the moon."

"Shut up, Harriet," Phelps groaned.

"Start the grill," Hoby said as he busied himself scrubbing the meat juice off his fingers.

"It's been started for three days," Harriet snapped.

"Get me some buns, tomatoes, and lettuce. You hungry, Mr. Phelps?"

"I'm starving."

"How about you, Mrs. Phelps?"

"Well, a hamburger surely would taste nice."

"How about you . . . uh?"

"You know my name by now."

"Harriet, you be civil or I'm gonna whack you!" Phelps said.

"Sure, I'd like a hamburger! I'm dying for a hamburger! There's nothing I'd like better than a fat, juicy hamburger!"

"Then get out four buns and four plates and all the fixings and set yourself down at the table."

Twenty minutes later they were chomping into the most delicious hamburgers they had ever tasted. They chewed and smacked and gulped, grease dribbling down their chins, bits of meat and mustard and bun sticking to their lips and fingers. Harvey moaned after the last bite disappeared between his teeth. Mrs. Phelps poured herself a second cup of coffee. "I believe I might consider going down on my knees if this were a fit place for worship," she sighed. Harriet gobbled every crumb off her plate; with a crust of bread she swabbed up the grease and chewed the crust slowly, her bright green eyes focused on Hoby's face.

"Feel better?" Hoby asked.

"Sure do. How can we ever thank you, Mr. Tibbs?"

"You're good folks. You run a wholesome place for hungry workers."

Hoby took his plate into the kitchen. When he came back out with the trophy bag, Harvey presented him with a fifty dollar bill.

"It's not much. It's just a fraction of a fraction of what you're worth to us, but I hope you'll accept it. You're a hell of a man, Mr. Tibbs. I wish there were more like you."

"Won't you please stay and meet some of the fellows when they come in?" asked Mrs. Phelps.

"Thanks, but I better go. I'm pretty shot. I think I need to put my head down somewhere."

"What you got in that bag?" said Harriet.

"Nothing."

"How come you got it with you then?"

"I'm looking for something to put in it."

"Bet I could find something for you."

Harvey shouldered his daughter aside. "Please stay," he pleaded. "The guys'd love to meet you."

"Thanks again, but I better slip on out. I've had my reward. You're a great bunch of folks."

At the door Harriet pushed her way in front of her father. "Maybe you'll let me look into your bag sometime."

Hoby tried to stare into her crackling green eyes, but her expression was so fierce he couldn't.

"Mebbe so," he said. "Mebbe so."

20

Hoby didn't get out of Ajo that day. He found a motel at the north end of town and checked in. A couple of beers and a nap followed. Around six he woke up with a roaring hunger, which he quenched in a cantina with three meat burritos and a dish of refried beans. Belching contentedly, he retrieved Otis from the room. With the creature tucked inside the trophy bag, he strolled along a slope of sand and gravel behind the motel that rose to the crest of a west-facing hill. The sun had settled behind the mountains, smearing the sky with bright orange streaks; a fleet of torpid clouds hung motionless over the peaks. Hoby settled against a rock; he lifted Otis out of the bag and propped him between his thighs. The town was to his left, the streets laid out at right angles; the corner lights were just beginning to wink on. South of town loomed the massive hulk of the copper-smelting plant, topped by a towering smokestack. A coil of greasy fumes erupted from the stack, streaming southwest on the sway of the prevailing wind toward the Mexican border.

"Pretty sunset, Otis," Hoby commented, pulling on a fat cigar. He scratched the soft brown head. The fur was finer than the softest chinchilla. "It's bigger than I thought," he murmured. "This hamburger stuff doesn't just apply to my someday wanting to own my own joint. It's got to do with people's lives and what it is exactly that makes them happy. It's got to do with the way they live and think, their expectations of the good life. I guess you could say it's got something to do with the American dream. And the dream, in this culture at least, is connected in some way with hamburger. Somewhere along the line, when you try and explain the dream, the subject of hamburger comes up. A hamburger means nourishment and a full belly, and a full belly is one of the prerequisites of the dream. Shoot, you can't dream good dreams if your belly ain't been properly filled."

He puffed the cigar and scratched Otis's head. The creature stood between his knees, balanced on its three-pronged feet, staring at the fading light.

"That's where you belong, isn't it, Otis? Somewhere out there. And I suspect once this job is finished, that's where you'll go back to. I shouldn't keep you cooped up like this in a stuffy little bag. You deserve a better fate than that after all you've done for me. You've made the difference in my life. It's you who's responsible for my success. Without you, I'd still be turning patties in Palm Desert. You changed all that, Otis. Not only have you guaranteed me the ticket to my own success, you've turned a modest gift into a legendary talent. I'm not just out here curing bad hamburger,

I've embarked on a crusade to keep this civilization afloat, to fend off the enemies that threaten to capsize it. You and me, Otis, with me the visible one, out front, on the point, and you transmitting energy from a secret place located way out back somewhere. You're the one, Otis, you're the true power. Without you, the bacteria would win out, and we, the people of America, would be the losers. Our hamburger would disappear, vanquished by clouds of voracious microbes, and we'd be reduced to eating bunny food, lettuce and carrots. You're the real hamburger savior. Someday the story will be told, and I'll be the one to tell it."

The light was gone from the western sky. Hoby ground the cigar butt in the sand and stood up, cradling Otis in his elbow, pressing his cheek against the warm, downy pelt. From inside the creature's body he could detect a pulse, a faint beat, slower than his own, a steady tick, indefatigable.

21

When he opened the door to his motel room, he got a shock. Harriet was in the bed, the sheet pulled up to her chin. Hoby jumped when he saw her, the trophy bag jerking in his hand. "How'd you get here?"

"I ain't lived here for fifteen years without acquiring a few friends."

"What are you doing here?"

"I come to pay my respects."

"Look . . . uh . . ."

"You know my name."

"I keep forgetting it."

"Get your clothes off, and get under the sheets, and I'll make sure you remember it."

"Now, listen . . . ah . . ."

"Harriet."

"Now listen, Harriet, if you don't leave right now, I'll call the manager."

"The manager's a friend of mine. If he comes in here, he'll most likely break a chair over your head for not giving me what I want. You ain't got a choice. So unbuckle your britches and hop on in here. I want to feel what it's like to have your hands against my flesh."

Hoby circled the room, undoing the buttons on his shirt. He pulled off his boots, then his socks. He tugged at his belt, taking his sweet time. His success as a hamburger healer had not enlivened his pace as a lover. He'd always been pokey when it came to that, wary as a possum crossing a busy intersection.

Harriet pulled the sheet down. Her body was compact and muscular. A body like a whip that could make a loud cracking sound. A lump rose in Hoby's throat as he gazed at her pouty nipples. He picked up his leather gun belt and strapped it around his waist.

"What's that for?" she called.

"I feel undressed without it."

"You're supposed to feel undressed when you get in bed with a woman."

"It gives me power. I always wear it when I have an important mission to perform."

She stared at him. "You don't seem that anxious to bed down. I know I'm not real pretty, but I do know how to make a man feel comfortable."

"I don't have many girlfriends," Hoby mumbled, almost apologetically, as he slid into bed.

"I like a man who's discriminating."

"In fact, I don't have any."

"I appreciate a man who holds himself back for the right moment."

Hoby adjusted the holsters so he could lie more comfortably. He smoothed the sheets and made sure the corners were tucked in. He grinned sheepishly. "I was married once, and one of the main complaints my wife had was my dilatory bedside manner."

"I think I understand."

"I'm basically shy. These holsters help me strut and swagger. Without them, I prefer to remain incognito."

"Why do you talk so much?"

"'Cause I live alone, and when you live alone the only person you got to talk to is yourself."

Harriet's warm, appealing mouth puckered into a pink knot. She gazed at him fervently, her eyes fixed and unblinking. "Put your hand here," she instructed.

Hoby had never had anyone look at him like that.

"There?" he croaked.

"That's right. Now pretend it's hamburger. Squeeze it."

"Like this?"

"Harder."

"I don't want to hurt you. My fingers are pretty strong."

"Put your fingers there. Right there. Do you chant or sing when you work?"

"Sometimes I hum."

"So hum."

"Hmmmm. Hmmmm."

"That's better. Your fingers are strong."

"They've had lots of practice."

"Do more of that."

"You feel lots better than hamburger."

"I'm not much firmer."

"Yes, you are. You're lovely. You've got a lovely body."

Harriet's eyes began to roll. "Hum some more," she said.

"Hmmmm. Hmmmm."

"Oh . . . Lord."

22

Twice during the night Hoby woke up to find himself locked inside Harriet, flaying her with his pelvis, being swung in return like a bag of suet in a high wind. The last time, it felt like he was trying to chin himself for a world's record. He made it up and over the rail in a final effort that rattled his toes and brought spittal frothing to his lips. Then he let go and fell into a pit lined with moss and old leaves. For a long time he lay there staring up at nothing, not moving, not breathing, trying to hear his heartbeat.

He woke up at six, his tongue stuck to the roof of his mouth. A glass of water helped, but his knees were rubbery and he fell back into bed. At seven he woke up again, mindful that he was due at the franchise in Douglas at midday. He tried to pack without making noise, but Harriet stirred anyway. "I'll buy you breakfast," she whispered.

"I better get going. I got an appointment at noon."

"You're really some kind of fire-spitting dragon."

"I have my moments. But it all depends upon the quality of the inspiration."

He finished packing and sat down on the edge of the bed. "I want to thank you very much. I needed you more than I realized. You were very good to me."

She scrutinized him carefully. His face was sweet and boyish, with a disarming smile. There was something serious and old-fashioned about him. Punctual, courteous, efficient. She imagined him doing the toast just right, poaching the eggs to perfection, never missing a payment at the bank. At the same time, underneath that smooth, genteel surface lurked a mania she had never encountered before, a weirdness that left her gasping.

"Will you be coming through again?" she asked.

"When I finish in El Paso, I'll drive back this way."

"Will you call me?"

"Sure. I'd like to call you."

Harriet yanked down the sheet. "Touch me. Touch me there."

"Where?"

"For Christ's sake, you know where!"

"Ah."

"Is it warm?"

"You bet."

"You can feel that it's warm, can't you?"

"Sure can."

"Remember that when you're on the road. Remember how you touched me there and how warm it felt."

"I won't forget, Harriet."

"You remembered my name!"

"Harriet. Harriet. Harriet."

"Say it again."

23

He stopped to gas up the Buick Skylark at a 76 station on the outskirts of Ajo. As he was kneeling to check the tires, he caught a movement out of the corner of his eye. A hatless man stood by the front bumper, dressed in tattered khakis, greasy, tangled hair dangling to his shoulders. A man of indecipherable age, black eyes glistening like olive pits in the folds of a sun-ravaged face.

Hoby shot air into the tire and stood up, coiling the air hose around the hook.

"You the fella they call the Ptomaine Kid?" The voice was intense and quavering.

Hoby went inside to pay. When he came out, the man was still standing at the bumper.

"You really think you can cure that hamburger?"

Hoby opened the door and placed one foot inside. The man's eyes looked as if they were about to pop from their sockets.

"You can't," he said. "It's too much to handle. You better forget about it."

"Says who?"

"Says me. The sickness goes way beyond the meat. It's everywhere. It's in everything."

"What sickness?"

"The taint. The taint. You know what I mean. You been sticking your nose in it everyday."

"I do what I can."

"Well, it ain't enough. Your efforts and all the efforts of all the other wizards in the world. It ain't nearly enough. The taint ain't just in the hamburger, you understand. It's in the grass and dirt. And once it's in there, it's damn near impossible to scrub out. But you know that. You done laid your hands on so much corruption these past few days, you ought to be an expert on that!"

"What are you, some kind of born-again weirdo?"

The man clenched his jaw and doubled up his fists. "I live in these parts," he declared. "I belong here."

"How do you know about me?"

"The whole town knows. You're a hero. You saved the hamburger for the copper miners. But you just watch. Next week, it'll be sour again."

A chill gripped Hoby's spine. "What makes you say that?"

"It ain't just the hamburger! That's what I'm telling you. It goes deeper than that."

"I think you're nutty."

"That's right. I am. That's what it takes to understand all this for what it really is."

Hoby swung into the car and pulled the door shut. The man drifted away from the bumper and stood several feet from the open window. "Did you ever wonder how come Harvey's meat went bad when he don't even belong to the WhammyBurger outfit? Didja?"

"Lots of independents are having trouble."

"But did you ever wonder?"

"Hamburger is suffering everywhere, fella."

"But the reason!" the man hissed. "Did the reason ever occur to you?"

Hoby started the engine.

"The taint's in the earth itself."

"I'm sorry. I have to go."

The man skittered toward the door. "You know where Harvey gets his meat from? Did you ever think of that?"

"No . . ."

"He gets it from Riverside, California. Same place WhammyBurger gets their meat."

"He gets his meat from there?"

"That's right."

The chill clamped tighter around his spine.

"Ain't that funny? Don't that make you want to laugh out loud?"

"If it were only true."

The man's face darkened. The eyes glared fiercely. "I'm not lying, mister. I'm too crazy to lie. You ask Harvey. Ask him."

"Okay. Maybe I will."

The man backed off, grinning fiendishly, stumbling over the island between the two pumps, hooting and cackling. "You do that first chance you git! You be sure and do that before you lay your fingers on another sick patty! You be sure and ask him that question!"

24

The Douglas franchise was in bad shape. Alfredo Reyes, the manager, was frantic with worry. For ten days he'd not served any hamburger. The customer load had dwindled to a few dozen a day, stalwarts who appeared mostly in the morning for coffee and sweet rolls.

"I know we're a scruffy little place down in the southeast corner of Arizona," Alfredo said. "But we're important to a lot of people here. And we're really important to my family and me, 'cause when the folks are buying I can make an okay living out of this place."

"All of the WhammyBurger outlets, whether they're located in Los Angeles or Douglas, Arizona, are important to us," Hoby said in his best corporate voice.

"You think you can help us, Mr. Tibbs?"

"I can try. There's not a franchise yet that I haven't turned around."

"Then let me show you the bad news."

It was worse than Hobby expected. In the fridge were three boxes of preformed patties, and every one of them, at least from what Hoby could discern, was infected.

"I think you ought to throw the whole lot out and start over," Hoby said.

"I've already done that. Last week I threw out better than two-score worth of patties, and for replacements I got these. They looked okay until the cooks fried them. Then they stank worse than an elephant fart. I can't throw this bunch away 'cause there's a clause in my contract that makes me liable for 40 percent of all unsold hamburger in stock. And that includes hamburger that goes unsold because of fire, theft, or spoilage."

Hoby looked at him. "I didn't know about that clause."

"It's pretty much standard throughout the organization. In the big cities, because of the higher volume, the liability percentage is even higher . . . 50, 60 percent. For us little guys, the numbers are more lenient. But it's still murder, no matter which way you cut it. I got a wife and three kids to take care of, plus my wife's mother and her crippled brother. Having more than a hundred uncookable hamburger patties on my hands poses a serious problem."

"Lamar really stuck it to you guys, didn't he?"

"Yeah, but I can't fault him the whole way for it," said Alfredo. "He lays out the initial investment on a highly perishable commodity, and he deserves a little protection at his end. Forty percent's a bit stiff, especially for a piddlyshit operation like the one I got here in Douglas. To be fair, I think he should scale it down to 25 or 30 percent. On the other hand, Lamar is pretty generous with the bonuses. If we make 10 percent over our annual volume quota, we get a $5,000 cash reward. That ain't bad. And that reward goes up with every additional 5 percent we tack on to the quota. So there're ways of making money in this business if you're willing to hustle. This ptomaine outbreak is a freak thing. Once it runs its course and things get back to normal, we'll be in the pink again."

"You don't think it's more serious than that? You don't think it might be more than a casual outbreak?"

Yesterday, Hoby would not have asked that question. But after listening to the spook in Ajo that morning, he was alert to the possibility that the problem might be more complicated.

"Mr. Tibbs, if I believed that, I would pack my pockets with rocks and jump into a deep well."

Hoby allowed the patties to thaw in units of two dozen at a time. Then he broke them into a pile and carefully and thoroughly sifted through each grain and bit, making sure all the microbes were eliminated. The work was tedious; by 7:00 he was bushed, his fingers stiff, the knuckles swollen.

"I'd better knock off, Alfredo," he sighed. "My hands are about ready to fall off. I'll be back in the morning at 9:00 sharp, and we'll finish up."

"I certainly appreciate everything you've done, Mr. Tibbs. I think we're off to a great start."

Hoby took a room at the Gadsden Hotel in downtown Douglas, a few blocks from the franchise. The evening was mild, with a soft breeze that dried the sweat on his cheeks as he drove with the windows down to the hotel. Douglas had a copper plant on the western edge of town. Fumes belched from the stack, blowing, under pressure of the prevailing wind, across the Mexican border.

After soaking his hands in a soothing compound of bath oil and club soda, Hoby poured a drink and telephoned Harriet.

"You're calling me so soon!" she gushed.

"I been thinking about you."

"How was the job today?"

He told her. He told her all about Alfredo Reyes and his problems. "Now, Harriet, I got a question to ask you."

"Fire away."

"I met a weird guy at the 76 station on the outskirts of Ajo this morning."

"That must have been Eddie Winerick," she interrupted. "Dressed like a wino? Hasn't had a bath in years? With eyeballs that turn off and on like headlamps?"

"That's him."

"Eddie Winerick cleans windshields at the stations along the strip to pick up extra coins. What did he say?"

"He told me your dad buys all his hamburger wholesale from the WhammyBurger distributors in Riverside, California. That's why your dad was having problems."

There was a pause. "Well, it's true," Harriet admitted. "I think Dad is the only independent in southern Arizona who has that kind of deal with a major franchise retailer."

"What are the terms of the deal, do you know?"

"No, I don't. I know Dad's had this contract for almost ten years, and up until the ptomaine outbreak he was happy with it. I think the franchise agreed to be his supplier in hopes that one day Dad would manage the WhammyBurger when it finally came to town. But Dad was too stubborn. He liked having his name over the door better'n someone else's. So when the franchise did come to town, it was Nelson Markley who became manager."

"Okay."

"Is there anything wrong?"

"I don't know. This whole hamburger business gets more complicated every day. Eddie Winerick was so insistent about the connection between your father's bad hamburger and the Riverside suppliers that it made me a little nervous. I don't really know what I'm supposed to be nervous about. I feel a little off-center is all. Maybe I been working too hard."

"I wish I was there to help you relax."

"Shoot, Harriet, I barely got enough strength to shampoo my hair. I'm glad you can't reach me."

"What about tomorrow?

"Tomorrow I'll feel different."

"You'll think about me then, won't you?"

"I sure will."

"About how much fun you had ironing out the wrinkles in this flabby old body?"

"Harriet, you're barely thirty-six years old. You don't have any wrinkles."

"About how you enjoyed pressing yourself against those wrinkles?"

"Harriet, I have to hang up now."

25

he next morning he was stepping across the lobby of the Gadsden Hotel, admiring the marble columns and pausing to punch his fingers against the tufted leather couches, when a sound made him look up, a hearty bellow. At the top of the marble stairs rising to the second floor, beneath a stained-glass representation of the glories of the copper-mining industry, a man lost his footing and with a protesting shout came tumbling down the hard steps like a log, rolling over and over, the shouts mounting in fury and surprise as he bumped down each step. With a crash and a jarring thump he reached the lobby floor. The impact settled him upright, arms and legs flared out, his mouth still working, a hoarse wheeze rattling between his lips.

Hoby ran over and knelt beside the man. He was dressed in an outlandish cowboy outfit: studded boots, sheep's-wool chaps, a sparkly sequined vest, a silk bandana tied at the neck. A ten-gallon hat tumbled the rest of the way down the steps, as if in pursuit of the head it had been resting on.

"Are you all right?" Hoby asked, gripping him by the shoulder.

"Rotten funging sumsabitches," the man growled, teetering on his haunches, then losing balance and landing on his elbow. The elbow gave way like a brittle strut. His head dropped toward the marble floor and might have struck it had not Hoby, with his quick hands, caught it like a softball. Then, doubled over, with his own face practically touching the floor, he pushed the man back up to a sitting position.

"Easy there, old-timer. Just sit still for a few minutes till you catch your breath. You took a nasty fall."

"Sumsafungingbitches," the man snarled. The hair bristled on his neck. His gray eyes fogged over with shock and rage. His cheeks sagged; his mouth was cracked and withered; his white hair swept up from his forehead in a striking pompadour, which by some miracle had survived the tumble without collapsing around his ears. He was a handsome old coot with the glamorous looks of a movie idol back in the days when a man's smile and the angle of his hairline were enough to guarantee him a meal ticket.

The desk clerk dashed across the lobby and skidded to a halt beside them. "Bob . . . Bob . . . you all right?" he cried.

"Goddamn funging steps!" The old man grabbed his hat. Reaching around while still in a sitting position, he thrashed the marble steps with the hat . . . thwap thwap thwap . . . cursing furiously.

"Stop it, Bob! Stop it right now!" the clerk scolded. "Aren't you supposed to be at the children's breakfast at 9:00?"

Bob looked up, pain and remorse registering in his bloodshot eyes; warm, expressive eyes despite the puffy folds surrounding the sockets.

"You are, aren't you? Pedro's coming to get you at 8:45, and here you are, drunk on your ass."

Hoby smelled the gin, a musty, perfumed fragrance mixed with sweat and damp sheep's wool. "Can I be of help?" he asked the clerk.

"Help me get him to his feet and into the café, and we'll try and get some coffee down him."

"He's supposed to be somewhere at nine?" Hoby grunted, tugging at the old man's armpits and managing finally, with the clerk's help, to get him to his feet.

"He's supposed to be at a special breakfast for the schoolchildren of Douglas this morning to sing songs and tell stories," the clerk replied. "But he can't go like this."

Chagrined, head down, unsteady, Bob, propped up on either side, tottered across the lobby. He was a big man, well over six feet tall, and it was all the clerk and Hoby could do to keep him upright. Another man, emerging from the café, rushed to help, getting a thumbhold in Bob's belt. Pushing, shoving, nudging, they steered the besotted man between the tables and plopped him down in a booth.

A cup of coffee appeared between his hands and a sweet roll next to his elbow. "Now you drink that, Bob, and you eat that roll, and by and by I'm gonna get you up and walking," the clerk snapped. "You're not gonna disappoint those kids if I can help it. They been waiting all week to hear you, and if you don't entertain them this morning, you can look for a new place to stay the night, 'cause you're not going to be staying here at this hotel. You hear me, Bob?"

Bob raised his ruined, craggy face. His eyes brimmed with cloudy tears. A salty drop detached itself from the corner of his left eye and dribbled down the leathery cheek and disappeared into the speckled mustache fringing his upper lip.

26

At the WhammyBurger franchise a few minutes later, Hoby pitched into his work. Several times during that long morning, when his fingers started to cramp, Alfredo Reyes rubbed his shoulders and massaged his wrists. Later, they had lunch together, alone in the kitchen. There wasn't much business, so Alfredo had dismissed most of the staff.

"You know what I think?" Alfredo asked, cooling his coffee with an ice cube. "I think we can attribute most of our troubles to our competitors."

"What do you mean?" Hoby was chewing the last of a breaded chicken sandwich.

"I think our competitors are jacking around with our product. Somebody's poisoning our meat. That's a fact. Why not point the finger at them? It makes sense."

"That's a pretty blanket accusation, Alfredo. How come, if they're deliberately soiling the meat, they're having the same problems we are?"

"Because they're doing it indiscriminately to make us think we all have the same problem. You wait and see. In a few weeks our competitors will be back in business, minus the healing benefits of the Ptomaine Kid. You mark my word. There's something devious going on here."

"Have you shared this theory with anyone else?"

"I telephoned Mr. Whammers yesterday and explained it to him."

"What did he say?"

"He said that he had had the same thoughts. He said he was worried that what was going on here in the Southwest wasn't so much an epidemic as it was a kind of war, a dirty war for control of one of our country's most important food resources."

"That's hard for me to believe," said Hoby. "That anyone would deliberately poison a hamburger crop for whatever reason."

"We live in a scary world, Mr. Tibbs. You are a healer, so you may not see it as clearly as I do. There are people out there who will do anything to put themselves on top. People who simply don't care what happens to others. People without compassion or feelings."

"But that's almost like a . . . a form of murder," Hoby said. "You start messing with what people eat, and you touch them where they are most vulnerable."

"Precisely. And if you can turn them away from one type of food to another, you can begin the slow but inevitable process of altering not only their habits but their way of thinking. We're talking about something really significant here, the effects of which we can't even begin to measure. I had a professor at Arizona State who used to lecture us about what the introduction of spices did to the European consciousness in the fifteenth and sixteenth centuries. Spices brought back from the Middle East by the Crusaders and later in larger, marketable quantities by Venetian and Portuguese merchants. It revolutionized the eating habits of many Europeans, especially those living along the Mediterranean. It spurred additional exploration around the tip of Africa and across the Atlantic. It was responsible, in part, for Columbus and, after him, Cortez and Pizarro. The effects were staggering. We're still feeling them today. And all because of a change in diet."

27

Hoby worked hard the rest of the day, and when the day was done all the patties in Alfredo Reyes's refrigerator were bacteria-free. Using Hoby's chemicals, Alfredo tested each patty. The results were negative. Alfredo raised his hands and let out a shout.

"The deeper I get into this, the more I think I'm going to spend my life traveling from franchise to franchise," Hoby groaned as he soaked his hands under the tap.

"You mean one visit doesn't do it?"

"One trip does fine for the hamburger in stock at the time. But what about the new batch when it arrives? Will it be polluted? If it is, I'm wasting my time chipping away at the symptoms. If it is a conspiracy like you suggest, I've got to find the source."

"The cattle," said Alfredo.

"That's correct."

"The biggest range I know of on which cattle graze exclusively for the WhammyBurger organization is in New Mexico."

"Outside Hatch? Along the Rio Grande?"

"Correct."

"Maybe I ought to go over there and look into the mouths of a few of the beeves."

"Maybe you ought to go to the packing plant at Deming and check their procedures," Alfredo suggested.

"I'm sure Lamar keeps close tabs on that. He's got Ralph Manning dogging my trail. Do you know Ralph?"

"Sure."

"What do you think of him?"

"He's helpful, courteous, efficient, professional. I've never had any trouble with him."

"I have," said Hoby. "Though for the life of me I can't quite figure out what it is."

28

That evening Hoby had dinner at Alfredo's—"insufficient payment," Alfredo declared, "for all you've done for my shop."

Before sitting down at the table, Hoby met the rest of the family—the wife, the three children, the crippled brother, the grandmother. They lived in two modest houses, one set behind the other on a deep plot of land in a secluded neighborhood. The grandmother and brother lived in the smaller house in the back, with Alfredo and his family occupying the one in front. In between there was a yard, kept tidy, all the toys picked up, the bicycles and Big Wheels clustered in a little parking area. A couple of olive trees provided shade and also served as support for a rope swing with a plastic seat. Along the south side of the smaller house was a garden, which already, in early June, was bearing vegetables. The interiors of both houses were handsomely furnished and spotlessly kept. The walls were covered with photographs of family members stretching back three generations, including one of the grandmother and her husband (deceased) taken in Chihuahua City in 1931. Their features and clothing were colored in by hand. An ornate oval frame banded the photograph.

The meal was delightful—shrimp from the Sea of Cortez, peppers and zucchini from their garden, rice and pinto beans from the *mercado* at that end of town. Hoby's contribution was a twelve-pack of Bohemia. The crippled brother—Alfredo's brother-in-law, bound to a wheelchair by a disfigured spine—was passionate about baseball. He wondered if Hoby, who lived in southern California, had ever seen the Angels or the Dodgers play. No, Hoby replied. Well yes, once, when he was in Anaheim . . . yes, he had seen the Angels. When the brother pressed him for details, Hoby confessed he couldn't remember; he was drunk at the time.

The brother scolded him for squandering such a marvelous opportunity. "I like to drink, too . . . beer, as you can see," he said, holding up his third bottle of Bohemia. "But I would never allow my appreciation of a major league baseball team to be obscured by too much liquor."

He sighed. "I have never seen a major league team. I have seen Mexican professionals play in Hermosillo, and once I went to Albuquerque to see the minor league team there. But a real major league team with real stars I have never seen. Can you tell me what Nolan Ryan is like? Was he pitching that night?"

Bettina Reyes, Alfredo's wife, steered the conversation away from baseball by asking Hoby why he thought he had been blessed with the gift of healing bad hamburger meat.

"I'm not sure," Hoby replied.

"Did God speak to you? Did you hear his voice?"

"No, no. It wasn't like that. It was more like a visitation. I heard no voices. But I was visited by someone, and after that everything changed."

The grandmother tipped forward in her chair. The brother looked up from his beer bottle.

"Someone? Who was this someone?"

"I'd rather not say. It's so private and personal that if I tell you, I might lose my power."

"*Un angel*," the grandmother whispered, her eyes widening. "*Lo que le paso fué un milagro.*"

"*Sí,*" Bettina nodded. "*Este hombre fue verdaderamente bendecido por Dios.*"

"Maybe you were hit on the head by one of Nolan Ryan's fast balls and when you woke up you thought you were in heaven," said the crippled brother.

"Hector, you have drunk too much beer," Alfredo said sternly.

"Forgive me," Hector said, his face crimsoning.

"Hector, someday I want you to come to California and I'll take you to Angels Stadium," said Hoby.

"You will?"

"Yes. And I won't have a drop to drink. We'll enjoy the game, we'll spend the night in a fancy motel, the next day we'll go to Disneyland."

Hector was ecstatic. "Maybe there will be an afternoon game! Maybe we could spend the night in the stadium! Maybe I could sleep with my head on the pitcher's mound!"

The party broke up soon after that. Alfredo offered to drive him to the Gadsden Hotel, but the night was warm and Hoby needed the exercise. He kissed Bettina and the grandmother, both of whom lingered over his hands, stroking his palms, rubbing their thumbs against the knuckles. He shook hands with Hector and told him he would send him an autographed photo of Nolan Ryan.

"But Nolan Ryan plays for the Houston Astros now," said Hector. "And you are not traveling in that direction."

"How about an autographed photo of Gene Autry?"

"He is only a rich man. He is not a baseball player. To be a baseball player is much better than being a rich man. How about Don Baylor? Or Minnie Minoso. Ah, Minnie Minoso! There was a baseball player."

Alfredo walked Hoby to the end of the block. He embraced him, thanking him for all he had done and for the honor of having dined with his family in their modest home.

The night air was smooth and velvety. The street was full of people, families mainly, out for a stroll, boys and girls on bicycles. The leaves of the live oaks rustled overhead. Bats and nighthawks swirled around the streetlamps. The stars hung in the sky like bits of sparkling foil. The Big Dipper was especially prominent, tilting forward on the western horizon, the handle soaring up toward the center of the galaxy.

Hoby walked on, thinking about the cigar waiting for him in his room at the hotel. So complete was his absorption he didn't notice the car following at a discreet interval, with its lights off and its engine humming in low gear.

29

The cigar could wait. Walking along Chiricahua Street, two blocks from the hotel, he paused in front of a tavern. The door was open. Most of the stools were occupied, one by a fellow who looked familiar.

It was an appealing tavern, despite the bilious green walls and plastic siding some fool had tacked onto the top of the pinewood bar. The walls were decorated with trophy heads—a moose head, a grizzly head, a coyote head, the head of an antelope with a bullwhip dangling from the prongs. The heads were coated with dust, the fur ratty and stained. Whoever mounted them had done so years ago when such trophies meant something, both to the people who bagged them and to those who displayed them. Behind the bar, over the mirror, was an illuminated advertisement for Cerveza Popé. It featured a U.S. cavalry officer digging a latrine trench at the edge of a Plains Indian village. The man was in full uniform; two warriors stood guard with Winchester rifles. The caption read: "Colonel Ranald Mackenzie Makes Amends for Having Destroyed the Comanche Horse Herds at Palo Duro Canyon."

"I think I owe you an apology. Or at least an explanation."

A five-dollar bill was being handed to the bartender in exchange for the shot of Old Crow Hoby had ordered. "You were especially helpful to me this morning, and I'd like to acknowlege that fact."

Hoby pinched the glass between his fingers and slugged back the juice. The fire started simultaneously at the top of his skull and in the pit of his belly. It spread deliciously through his abdomen, down his throat, meeting at his heart, which, like an automobile engine on a frigid day, kicked reluctantly into gear.

"Do that again," the man said to the bartender, pointing at the empty shot glass.

"I was worried you might have hurt yourself," Hoby said. "Marble steps are no fun to bounce down."

"I'm always falling," the man confessed. "I'm getting too old to drink and walk. My name's Bob Pringle. What's yours?"

"Hoby Tibbs."

"The Ptomaine Kid."

"How'd you know?"

"One good cowboy imposter can always spot another. Who else would wear a brace of empty holsters strapped to his waist?"

"After a hard day on the range, I need a warm spot to tuck my hands into."

"I know what you mean."

Hoby relaxed his face into an amiable expression. "I was thinking this morning that your face looked familiar."

"How old are you?"

"Forty-one."

"Where did you grow up?"

"Pomona, California."

"Then you most likely saw me once or twice. I used to do a lot of horse operas for Republic Studios back in the 1940s. *Crimson Spurs, The Pecos Kid, Bilyeu Punches Through*. A bunch of 'em."

"Shoot, yes . . . of course."

"Later on they talked me into doing those godawful singing westerns. You remember when Roy Rogers and Gene Autry were big? I could always sing, had a pleasing tenor voice. And by a crackling fire, under a full moon, with cattle lowing and a woman's lips fastened to my thigh, I could sing about as pretty as you'd ever want to hear."

"Cowboy Bob Pringle!"

"You got it, pardner. In the flesh. After a lifetime of profligacy and dissolution, still the meanest hombre this side of the Gila River."

"Well, I'll be damned. I saw a lot of your movies when I was a kid . . . *Val Verde, Navajo Tears, The Return of the Dog-Faced Boy.*"

"Yep. I made 'em all. Some I liked, some I couldn't stand. Some whose message I agreed with, others that made me puke. We couldn't put those shows out fast enough. Back in 1949, seeing a cowboy movie on a Saturday afternoon for a lad of ten in the United States of America was about as close to paradise as he was going to get."

"So what are you doing now, Bob? I see you got a guitar."

"Now I'm retired. I travel from town to town, mainly Arizona and New Mexico, doing a few benefits, singing in restaurants, entertaining old friends and a few new fans. That's why I got this with me tonight," he said, holding up the guitar. "I did a couple of numbers in a restaurant down the street. It's a sweet life, except when I duck into my cups at 8:30 in the morning. I can't seem to resist that gin. Some mornings I get up, fully intending to make it a productive day, and the sight of a bottle of Beefeaters sitting on the bureau proves irresistible. Down goes the gin, and out I go like a light. Though some mornings like this morning, I get dressed and go down to the street and make a public spectacle of myself."

"You look a whole lot better this evening than you did this morning."

"I feel better, thanks. And even though I'm in a bar, you'll be glad to know I'm abstaining."

"What's in the glass?"

"A mixture of club soda, grenadine, and a dash of bitters."

Hoby made a face.

"At my age it facilitates the digestive track. It gives me the illusion that I'm drinking the real thing."

Bob's eyes were clear. His cheeks had a pinch of color. He'd combed his silky white hair into a dashing pompadour. Despite his age, which Hoby guessed was around sixty-five or seventy, the remnants of a once-handsome face could still be detected through the puffy flesh around his eyes and jaw. The mouth in particular—tilted up in an easy, languid grin—was warm and appealing.

"How are you doing on your errand of mercy?" Bob asked.

"Not bad. Well enough, I guess. Although the hamburger issue grows more complicated every day."

"I don't touch the stuff anymore. Bad for the ticker."

"But good for the soul," Hoby countered. "The ultimate all-American comfort food. Every now and then you just got to have one."

"I know, I know. But at some point you got to weigh all the factors and make a decision. My arteries are pretty well clogged by all the junk I've devoured in my life. I had to make a choice, son. It was either gin or hamburgers, and I chose gin."

Hoby laughed and ordered another shot. He and Bob talked awhile, then Hoby stood up. "I got a job in Wilcox tomorrow and one in Lordsburg after that," he said.

"A cowpoke's work is never done," Bob sighed. "Soon as the sun sets, it rises somewhere else, and it's back in the saddle for the poor, weary guy. No one said it was easy."

"I don't remember you being so philosophical in your movies."

"When the camera's pointed at you, you got to move, not talk." Bob said. "Speaking of moving, I'll be doing that real soon if I pull another caper like I did this morning."

"You hang around here most of the summer?"

"Naw. I usually escape into Mexico. Got a place in Durango, up in the mountains."

"Are you up early? I'd like to see you again before I take off. Maybe we could have breakfast together."

"Drunk or sober, I'm up at 6:30 every morning."

"Shall we meet at the hotel café?"

"Sounds great, partner. I'd like that."

"Stick to bitters and grenadine tonight," Hoby advised.

"You can count on it. I'll wake up with a clear head and a stiff pecker. What is tomorrow anyway?"

"Wednesday."

"Yep. That's the day I get my hard-on. I'll have to stay sober to celebrate the event. At my age, it only happens once a week."

30

Hoby was a half-block from the tavern and had just stepped off the curb near the entrance to an alley when he heard a groan. He halted and peered into the alley. It was murky, the lights from the street penetrating a few feet into the narrow passageway. Trash cans lined the walls, heaped with refuse. A cat sprang out and glided into the shadows.

"Help . . . please . . . help."

Squinting, trying to see past the barrels, Hoby stepped into the gloom. The glow from the streetlights faded; the shadows congealed into a forbidding smudge. He fumbled a step or two, then came up short, his heart clacking between his teeth. Wedged between a pair of barrels, his face streaked and bruised, was a man, his body crumpled into a contorted posture.

Hoby went down on one knee for a closer look. The man's hand shot out and gripped him by the shirt collar, yanking him off balance. Hoby fell forward over the man's knees, choking and gasping as the fingers scuttled from his collar to his throat. The next instant another man reared up from behind a trash can and kicked at Hoby, trying to cave in his ribs; the kick clobbered his hip, a puncturing blow with the toe of the boot that flipped Hoby over on his back. The attackers were on him, one with his fingers gripping Hoby's throat, the other flailing at his face and neck with his fists. For a moment he lay there, too stupefied by shock and bewilderment to retaliate. Then his legs shot up, his knee catching one attacker in the back. Twisting and writhing, Hoby tried to break loose, rolling on one side just as the second attacker slammed his knee against his shoulder and groped for the fingers of his left hand. When he felt the fingers of his right hand start to bend back toward his wrist, Hoby let out a shriek. Pain shot up his arm, rattling his brain, convulsing his eyes with lurid explosions of color.

He heard another cry, a roar of furious rage, followed by a splintering crash as a large oval object exploded against the back of one attacker's head. Strips of polished wood fragmented around the man's skull, followed by a dull honking strum. The attacker pitched forward, loosening his grip. Hoby tried to roll to his left, but the other attacker had pinioned his wrist under his knee and was attempting to smash Hoby's fingers with a brick.

Before he could slug the man with his free hand, the oval object, trailing bits of wood and catgut, whipped around with a slushy hiss and smashed the second attacker in the side of the head, showering splinters and bits of wire. The hold on his left wrist loosened; Hoby shoved the stunned man off balance. Coiling his legs beneath him, he sprang over the man's body, his momentum carrying him out of reach of the boot of Cowboy Bob Pringle, which drilled directly into the attacker's groin. The man let out a strangled cry. Hoby rolled to his feet and reeled against a trash can, knocking it over with a crash.

"Let's get out of here," Bob panted, clutching the shattered neck of the guitar.

Gongs and whistles rifled the air as Hoby directed a final kick at the attacker, but Bob pulled him away and the kick went astray. Hoby's foot glanced off a barrel; the momentum wheeled him around in the direction of the street. Clutching one another, gasping, wheezing, their bodies crackling with adrenaline, Bob and Hoby stumbled out of the alley.

31

Bob went to the front desk in the lobby of the Gadsden Hotel to collect Hoby's room keys, while Hoby hung back in the shadow of a marble column. "Message for Mr. Tibbs," the clerk said, handing over the keys and a slip of paper. In the elevator Hoby read through swollen eyes that Harriet had called and wanted him to call her back.

"You look like you ran into a mountain," Bob said.

"I b'lieve I might have."

Hoby stretched out on the bed in his room while Bob telephoned room service for ice and aspirin. Otis was out of the trophy case, sitting on the windowsill behind the curtain, out of sight. Hoby groaned and stared up at the ceiling. His face ached, his hip was sore, his chest and shoulders were marked with red welts. Sharp pains ran up and down his wrists and fingers.

"What're you drinking?" asked Bob.

"There's a bottle in the top drawer."

The bellhop brought the ice, and Bob plunked some cubes in a glass and poured in a generous slug of Old Crow. He poured an additional measure for himself and tossed it down. Then he went into the bathroom and made a compress out of ice cubes and a washcloth. With that resting on Hoby's face, he took another snap of Old Crow.

"How d'ye feel?" he asked.

"Like shit."

"You want a doctor?"

"Don't think so."

"Anything broken?"

"No. I'm just sore. Man, am I ever sore."

"They were looking to do bad things to your body."

"Thank God you came along, Bob."

"I was walking past the alley when I heard you yell. I knew your voice. It sounded like they were trying to drive a stake into your heart."

"Sorry about your guitar."

"I'll pick up another tomorrow." Bob took Hoby's glass and refilled it. "How you feeling now?"

"I think I'm gonna get sick."

"Have at it."

While Hoby was vomiting in the toilet, Bob filled the tub with warm water and helped Hoby, who was shaking all over, into it. "You're in shock, son. Get yourself in the water and lie still and you'll feel better."

Hoby tried to keep the tears from leaking out. He bit down on his lip and squintched his eyes to slits, but the pain from the welts marking his face forced him to relax his muscles, and the tears came rolling down.

"They were after my hands, Bob."

"Well, son, they're your primary asset. If somebody wants to put you out of business, that's where they're gonna go."

Hoby sank deep into the tub till the water lapped his chin. "Who would want to break my hands?"

"It seems to me," said Bob, "and this might sound a mite cynical, but it seems to me your competition might have an interest in doing that."

"How come?"

"It's not hard to figure. You been going around the Southwest curing the WhammyBurgers and getting lots of publicity for it. Meanwhile, the hamburger is still suffering. You leave town, and WhammyBurger goes back to business. Right away, folks flock in to satisfy their craving. WhammyBurger gets all the business, while the other places are forced to keep their doors shut."

Hoby stopped shaking. His stomach quieted down. "It makes sense, I suppose. But I'm a healer, Bob. I'm here on an errand of mercy. I don't want to hurt anyone. I want to help. Once I get done with the WhammyBurger outlets, I'll help the others."

"I know, son, but a lot of people don't see it that way. They see only that you're not helping them. And they don't understand that. Especially when there's money to be made."

Hoby stepped out of the bath, dried off, and slipped into bed. Bob put cold compresses on his chest and forehead. "The phone message from Harriet," he said.

"Right."

"She said it was urgent."

"Can you dial the number for me?"

Harriet's voice was loud and squawky. "Hoby, I wouldn't of bothered you if I didn't think it wasn't important. A fellow named Ralph Manning was here today, checking on our hamburger. He left a piece of paper in the kitchen that's kind of puzzling. None of us can make any sense of it. It's got some formulas on it, some writing, and a map of New Mexico with some towns underlined. The writing says 'Call Beaky tomorrow about the load.' Then there's a phone number. There's something else too, a statistic that reads '426 mixed Charolais and Angus.' Does that mean anything to you?"

"No."

"Are you all right?"

"Sure. I'm just tired."

"I think you ought to see this paper."

"Did Ralph leave it, or did it fall out of his briefcase?"

"It fell out, I guess. The cat was in the kitchen, and I didn't want Mr. Manning to see him there, what with the health regulations being what they are, so I was trying to shoo him out . . . the cat, I mean . . . when his foot got stuck to this paper that had slipped under the cutting table. I ran around to the front to catch Mr. Manning and give him the paper, but he had already left. I checked all the motels along the strip, but he wasn't in any of them. I guess he drove on to Tucson. What should I do with the paper? Mr. Manning may need it."

Hoby sat up in bed, his fingers tightening around the telephone. "Send it to me."

"I could get in the car and deliver it to you."

"No. You better mail it to me."

"You don't want to see me?"

"Of course I want to see you, Harriet. I'm dying to see you. A lot has happened these past few days. I can't tell you about it now."

"Are you okay?"

"Sure. I'm fine. I been learning some new things about the business."

"I wish you'd drive over here and pick up the paper in person."

"I can't, Harriet. I'm too tired to drive. I can't take the day off. Why don't you just mail it to me? Care of the WhammyBurger franchise in Lordsburg, New Mexico."

"Daddy wants to talk to you, too." Her voice was tight and thin.

"Have him call me."

"It's the kind of conversation that's better to have face-to-face."

Hoby grew quiet.

"He used to know Lamar Whammers a long time ago."

"Oh?"

"Right after the Korean War when Daddy got out of the Air Force, he worked for Mr. Whammers in St. Louis before Mr. Whammers moved to California."

"And what do you think your dad has to say about Mr. Whammers?"

"I don't know, Hoby. He won't tell me. He just said it was personal and that you might find it of interest."

"How come he didn't tell me when I was in Ajo?"

"He hadn't seen that piece of paper then. He says he thinks he knows what's going on."

Hoby's heart flopped like a fish on a dry dock. "I'll be there tomorrow," he said.

"Call Cochise Airways. They have a morning flight. At least they used to."

"I'll call right now."

"Call me back and I'll pick you up at the airport."

"Great. I appreciate this, Harriet."

"I miss you, Hoby. I been thinking about you since you left. You're my dragon. I like it when you breathe fire in my face."

Hoby returned the phone to its cradle. He lay back on the bed and looked up at the paint flaking and peeling from the ceiling.

"So we're off to Ajo tomorrow?" Bob said, filling Hoby's glass with fresh ice.

"You don't have to go."

"There are two guys in this town tomorrow morning who're gonna have sore heads. And when they remember who it was that gave them those sore heads, they're gonna want to get even. You think I want to hang out here by myself?"

"I'm glad you're coming, Bob."

"Every cowboy imposter needs a sidekick. I had one named Jake in a couple of movies. Jayhawker Jake, from Junction City, Kansas. He was a good man to have on your side when the going got rough."

"You got a gun, Bob?"

"No, I don't. They scare me. I gave mine up one night after I fired it at a burglar and killed my favorite dog. Shot him right through the neck. A .32 automatic, of Czech manufacture. A nice gun, but tempermental. No, son, when I get put out with people today, I just pick up my glass and move to another table. Now what did she say the name of that airline was?"

32

On the way to the airport in Hoby's dusty four-door Buick, Bob asked to stop by a music store. "I don't play the guitar much anymore," he confessed. "But I kinda like to keep one handy."

It was a flawless morning. The sun beamed through an azure sky, outlining the mountains in a translucent light. The airport was located a couple of miles north of Douglas. They arrived at the squat adobe terminal, huddled under a trio of swishy tamarisk trees, a few minutes before nine. Since they would only be gone for the day, they brought no luggage other than Bob's new guitar, which had set him back fifty bucks. Hoby offered to pay, but Bob said no.

Bob wore tan slacks, a matching jacket, and a kelly-green sports shirt. Hoby wore his everyday clothes—a pair of khakis, tattered at the cuffs; a blue cotton shirt with the sleeves rolled up to the elbows. He had left his holsters back in the room at the Gadsden Hotel along with Otis, out of sight in the trophy case, away from the prying eyes of the chambermaids. He felt skittish, on edge, his body still recoiling from the effects of last night's altercation. His face was splotched with bruises. When he tried to chew a stick of gum, a stabbing pain shot through his gums. For the umpteenth time that morning, he ran a finger around his mouth to make sure all his teeth were there.

"And where are you gentlemen going today?" the agent behind the counter at Cochise Airways asked.

"Ajo."

"Together?"

"Correct."

"And you will be returning?"

"This afternoon."

Stamp stamp, click click, scratch scratch . . . Hoby had the tickets in his hand. Bob offered to pay his half, but Hoby shook his head. "My treat. I appreciate the company."

"Your face looks familiar, sir," the agent remarked. A wave of chaff-colored hair reared up off his pimply forehead like a floppy pancake. "Could I know you from somewhere?"

Hoby's right eye was swollen, his cheeks bruised; an ugly knot stuck out from the side of his jaw. He started to shrug when Bob butted in. "Not unless you ran into him in an alley last night. Were you messing around downtown in an alley last night?"

"No, sir. I was home in bed by 9:00."

"Then you probably never seen this fellow before."

"No . . . ah . . . I guess not. I guess you're right."

"You got to protect your privacy, son," Bob grumbled as they stepped out of the terminal and proceeded toward the aircraft parked on the apron.

Hoby's attention was distracted by the sight of the aircraft parked beyond the gate. A squat, chunky aircraft with a tail wheel and fixed landing gear, the two wing wheels skirted with metal flaps. Three engines, two on the wings, one in the nose, provided locomotion. Tipped back, with the fuselage slanting at an angle, the aircraft resembled a duck stuck to a patch of ice by its tail feathers.

"Good morning, gentlemen," the pilot said as he took their tickets. "Beautiful morning for a flight."

A young fellow, mid-thirties, wearing a cap with a brim that shadowed his steady gray eyes, a uniform jacket with COCHISE AIRWAYS stitched across a pair of wings above the lapel pocket. His features were refined and sculpted. He belonged to a breed known as Aviator Monks, a clandestine organization. They enjoyed getting high for pleasure and necessity, a fundamental need to merge their self-perception with a wider vision. They operated mainly in the Caribbean and Canada. A few had recently arrived in the American Southwest. They were crack pilots, primarily of propeller-driven planes. They had no families. They never married. They took vows of poverty and chastity. The aircraft was their mistress, the sky their medium, the birds their sole companions. They could fly anywhere in anything, and they did so primarily for the purpose of getting airborne so they could view the landscape from an elevated position. Their credo was a Cheyenne warrior maxim, which they carried on a laminated card tucked into the left breast pocket over their hearts:

> "They say an eagle can take in
> nearly the whole world with his
> eyes and see it as clearly as a man
> looks at the ground by his feet."

In Canada they followed the caribou and moose, in the Caribbean the soaring motions of the frigate bird, the paths of migrating whales. They were jovial and courteous, friendly and efficient. They enjoyed their work. Their work was their life. They wore their hair short. Their flesh tones were vibrant. They looked ordinary, except for their eyes. Their eyes indicated that they belonged to another order. Accustomed to looking at boundless horizons for long periods, their eyes were slow to focus on particulars. Their eyes looked past other people, not grudgingly or impolitely but out of a basic urge to see more than the human figure could offer. Their eyes hungered for landscape.

Hoby shook the aviator's hand. His grip was easy and relaxed. Hoby felt his scalp prickle as he looked into his eyes. His heart raced like a lawn-mower engine. Otis had eyes like that.

"Where did you get this heap?" Hoby asked.

"Isn't she a beauty? She's made of wood, with metal rudders and ailerons. The wheel struts are metal, the spats as well. The wings are made of wood, polished and sanded to form an ample roundness to provide the proper lift and airflow."

"It's Italian, isn't it?" asked Bob.

"That's right, sir. A Savoia-Marchetti 73. Originally built in 1935 as a commercial airliner for Alitalia, later adopted for war work in Ethiopia and Spain. We found her in Ecuador three years ago."

"Does she fly?" Hoby asked nervously.

"She flies like a dream, smooth and elegant in these mountain updrafts."

"It looks like it belongs in a museum."

"Oh no, sir. Not at all. A classic design like this is never dated. She's as airworthy as a condor. Her groundspeed is around 200 mph. She's steady and reliable. She can go and go and go."

The interior was snug—two lines of seats, six on each side of the narrow aisle. With the propellers gunning at full rpms, the aircraft trundled down the runway. There was no copilot; Hoby sat in the seat next to the pilot. The nose bobbed. The wheels bounced. The pilot hauled back on the wheel, pressing the rudders with the soles of his bare feet. The craft soared into the sky, motors roaring, the sun gleaming off its wings.

"Beautiful old bird! Beautiful old bird!" the pilot crooned. A pair of earphones crooked around the top of his head. His face looked as radiant as a cherub's.

"This baby flew missions in Ethiopia, Spain, Albania, Greece, Crete, and North Africa during World War II. She was shot full of holes. She had two engines blow up on her, her rudders knocked out, but she never crashed."

Clusters of gritty-dark mountains rose up, stark and isolated. Arroyos and ravines slashed the slopes between thickets of sage and cholla and saguaro cactus. Cultivated patches splashed the washes at their widest points. Smooth chunks of florescent red rock shouldered up through the sparse soil.

Fifty minutes later they came in for the landing at Ajo. The soft, manicured fingers of the aviator-monk caressed the throttles and trim tabs. Down, down the aircraft bumped and shivered, the fixed wheels reaching out to make contact with the warm, welcoming earth.

33

arriet met them and drove them to the diner. The sight of Hoby's beat-up face upset her. When he wouldn't tell her what happened, she got mad and pulled the car over to the curb.

"You better 'fes up to the lady," Bob advised.

"All right . . . all right. I got punched out in an alley last night by two mugs looking to put my hands out of commission. If it hadn't been for Bob Pringle and his samurai guitar, I'd be in the hospital now."

Harriet groaned. She lit a cigarette, snorting streams of smoke. "What's going on?" she muttered. "How come hamburger's becoming such a battleground?"

"I don't know. Let's go see your dad."

"It reminds me of picking a scab," she continued. "Remember when you were a kid and you had a scab form over a cut, and after a few days you'd pick at it and peel it back, and there under the crust the wound looked just as bad as it did when it first opened, maybe worse? Well, that's what this hamburger business is getting to be. You pick at the scab long enough, and you're going to uncover something really ugly."

"I think the lady's a poet," Bob said.

They reached the diner at 11:00. The smokestacks of the copper-smelting plant belched black, greasy fumes, away from the town. The day shift wasn't due in for lunch until noon, so Hoby and Harvey Phelps had time to talk. The day was warming up. After greeting Bob and Harriet, Harvey led Hoby to a picnic table under a paloverde tree in the dusty back lot of the diner. The air stank. Hoby wrinkled his nose. He sipped from a cold bottle of Coke. Harvey had a cup of coffee. Bob remained inside the air-conditioned diner with Harriet and Mrs. Phelps.

"I appreciate your coming back here, Mr. Tibbs."

"Call me Hoby."

As they crossed the back lot to the picnic table, Harvey's limp became more pronounced. "You get that in the war?" Hoby asked.

"The Korean one . . . yeah. I was a gunner in a twin-engine B-26, and I caught a piece of shrapnel in my left foot on a mission over the Yalu River."

"That must've stung."

"Only for about ten or twelve years. Then the pain went away."

Harvey's skin, white and pasty, glistened like the marbling on a cheap steak. He ran his fingers through the bristle of an old-fashioned flattop. "Maybe you better give this a look." He unfolded the sheet of paper and flattened it out on the picnic table.

It was just as Harriet described. There was a map, a few formulas, a telephone number, and a note addressed to somebody named Beaky—all written on a sheet of typing paper with what appeared to be a black felt-tip pen.

"Ralph called last night wanting to know if I found it."

"What did you say?"

"I told him I hadn't. I told him I looked all over the place and couldn't locate it. He sounded upset."

"How come you did that, Harvey?"

Harvey took a deep drag off his cigarette and leaked the smoke between his teeth. "'Cause I'm tired, Hoby. I'm tired of having to make deals in order to make a goddamn living. I'm ready to join the Apaches. I'm ready to eat mesquite beans for the rest of my life."

"Harriet told me you knew L. G. Whammers back in another life."

"That's right, I did. It's a long story, and maybe you better hear some of it before I say anything else. It all began when he was flying submarine reconnaissance patrols out of Puerto Rico. This was back in 1943 or '44. Lamar was a first lieutenant, attached to the Sixth Army Air Force Base on the island of Antigua. One day while on leave in the Dominican Republic, he met up with Ramfis Trujillo. The two took an instant liking to one another. Lamar was a poor boy from Arkansas, but he had one thing going for him. He was the legitimate cousin of an Arkansas congressman, the honorable Lucas J. Eichorn, who also happened to be chairman of the House International Relations Committee. On the strength of that connection, Ramfis introduced him to his father—the big jefe down there—Generalissimo Rafael Leonides Trujillo Molina, absolute dictator of the 3 million citizens of the Dominican Republic. The meeting was successful. Trujillo liked Lamar. He especially liked the way Lamar referred to his congressional kin as 'Uncle Luke.'

"Well, Lamar wrote a few letters to Uncle Luke, full of praise for his new friends. Congressman Eichorn was impressed. Back then, the Good Neighbor Policy was in full swing. The Roosevelt administration was eager to do all it could for its Latin American allies. In return for an increase in appropriations, Trujillo offered Lamar the job as commander of the Dominican Air Force. Once his discharge became effective, Lamar accepted, and right after the war, in 1946, he moved to Santo Domingo. Back then, the Dominican Air Force didn't consist of much, a couple of medium bombers and a half-dozen P-47 Thunderbolts. To demonstrate his enthusiasm for the new job, Lamar led several strafing raids on Haitian cane cutters who strayed over the border from their side of the island. The raids were successful, and Lamar was personally decorated by Trujillo."

Harvey paused to light another cigarette. "I guess it was in 1950 or '51 that Lamar met Isleta Pearlman. She was a wealthy divorceé from St. Louis, vacationing in Havana, when Lamar ran into her. He fell for her like a steel anchor. Isleta had everything Lamar ever wanted in a woman— money, brains, good looks, long legs. With Ramfis's support, Lamar went after her like a coon dog. He took her to expensive nightclubs and on long horse-drawn rides through the streets of Havana. Old Man Trujillo gave Lamar whatever he needed to fuel his pursuit. Once the prey was treed, Lamar resigned his command and told the jefe he was returning to America. Trujillo didn't sweat it; in a country where his fingers reached literally into every pocket, he didn't have to worry about the loss of a few coins. Lamar remained a valuable contact for him.

"I first met Lamar in 1953, in St. Louis. He'd just married Isleta Pearlman, and I'd just gotten back from Korea. He took a liking to me 'cause I'd been in the Air Force and got shot up. Lamar had a soft spot for guys in airplanes who had the misfortune to get shot up.

"Back then, he was looking to invest some of Isleta's money in a profitable business. Automated food machines had just been invented, and employers in big offices were installing them. The workers liked them. They were a real novelty. For a dime, a guy on the line could get a cup of coffee and a doughnut. He could eat it right there while taking a short break, before getting back to work. The machines were efficient and cost next to nothing to operate. They soon became so popular they eliminated the function of the little guy who used to come around the office or factory with a cart full of coffee and doughnuts and other things. These carts were usually operated by handicapped war vets who obtained the coffee and doughnuts from the government at a very low price. The carts were awkward. Sometimes they banged into the machinery. The factory owner was liable for the little guy if anything happened to him or his cart. So the little guy had to go to make room for the food machines. You don't have to pay insurance on a food machine.

"Well, Lamar wanted to get into the business real bad. There was money to be made, and Lamar got very excited about that. I was one of the fellows he hired to go around to various plants and suggest they install a few of his machines on the premises. The idea was well received. The timing was right; the idea and the technology came together in a neat package. Business was pretty hot for about a year. Of course, there were a few employers who resisted, who liked the idea of the little guy coming around with his cart full of coffee and sandwiches and glazed doughnuts. But Lamar put the pressure on, and they soon relented."

"What kind of pressure?" Hoby asked.

Harvey stared down at the cigarette fuming between his fingers. "Even after all these years, I'm reluctant to admit it. It was a little thing compared to the amount of bombs we dropped on Pyongyang or the villages we used to shoot up just for kicks on the way home from a mission. But Lamar always had a knack for putting his finger on the jugular. He's a kind of genius that way."

"Come on, Harvey, let's hear it. If this is confession time, I want it all."

Harvey looked over at the copper plant, then back down at his hands. They were big hands, the fingers like rolls of twisted dough with the tips squared off.

"We beat 'em up, Hoby. We took their carts and smashed them. And we took their crippled bodies and squeezed them till they begged us to stop."

The bruises on Hoby's face began to throb.

"There wasn't a lot of them. Maybe a half-dozen in all. One old boy I remember in particular. He'd been gassed in the Argonne during Big War

Number One. When he got excited his lungs churned like butter in a crock. He fought like an animal. We damn near destroyed his apartment before we pinned him down. He had trouble walking after that. Couldn't breathe very well either. He was a tough old bird. Been decorated at Belleau Wood. Silver Star for bravery."

"So you were a goon, Harvey. Just like the two guys who hammered on me last night."

"That's right, Hoby. I came out of the war a mean-ass bastard. It's a hard adjustment to make, between wartime and peacetime. They teach you how to kill, put you in a uniform, tell you that it's okay to kill, and send you off to the battlefront where you can kill and kill and kill. You do the job. After awhile you get pretty good at it. I got so I could really mess up a North Korean village with the pair of .50 calibers at my disposal. It was kinda fun. Then suddenly the war's over, and you're out of uniform, and you can't kill anymore. It's a hell of an adjustment."

"Did Lamar reward you for your muscle?"

A light wind dispersed the veil of smoke wreathing Harvey's troubled face. "Sure. We were a big success. We had a great track record in St. Louis. We started in Kansas City and ran up against the Mafia there. They had most of the jukeboxes in town, and naturally when the food machines came out, they wanted those too. And they got them. The Kansas City boys can be very persuasive when they need to. We moved into a few plants in the Fairfax area, but that's all. The guinea bastards ran us out of town faster than a wad of spit can travel in a cyclone."

"Did they get rough?"

"Not really. They didn't have to. One afternoon they paid a courtesy call on Lamar at his estate in Ladue. Three guys, dressed in sharkskin suits and wing-tip shoes. They told Lamar what they'd do to Isleta if he didn't lay off. You never saw Isleta, but she was a knockout. They never raised their voices, they never used foul language. They just described in minute detail what they'd do to her face and body if Lamar didn't pull out."

"What happened?"

"Lamar pulled out, lock, stock, and barrel. He lost interest in food machines and moved to California. This must've been around 1956 or '57. California was the fastest-growing state in the union. Right away he went into the hamburger business. A few well-entrenched interests wouldn't let him open up in Santa Monica or Burbank, so he had to be content with locations on the suburban fringes. He was patient and crafty, cultivating the right contacts and writing in contractors for a percentage of whatever franchise they constructed. Within five years he had established two dozen WhammyBurger outlets in the greater Los Angeles area. By 1965, there were operations in San Diego and Ventura and as far east as Needles and Blythe. WhammyBurger, Inc., had become the second-largest hamburger franchise in the state.

"Now, Lamar was always good to me. He remembered me and asked me to move to Riverside to help organize the franchise headquarters. But I wanted to live in Arizona with the Mexicans and the Indians and the cholla and the lizards. He offered me a franchise anywhere I wanted—Yuma, Phoenix, Flagstaff, Tucson. But I didn't want to be a manager. I wanted to be an owner. I wanted to own my own place and have my name up over the door. You know . . ."

"Sure, sure. I know."

"Lamar was very understanding. He said he'd supply my hamburger wholesale, even though I wasn't a franchise member. For old time's sake. And for a better price than any supplier in Tucson or Phoenix could offer. So here I am, in business for myself, with lots of sick hamburger and lots of strange memories."

Hoby took the slip of paper out of Harvey's hands, folded it carefully, and tucked it in his shirt pocket. "You got any idea what this is about?"

"I have my suspicions."

"What are they?"

"I'm not gonna tell you, Hoby. Even if you get mad at me, I'm not gonna tell you."

"Why not?"

"I believe in what you're doing. I believe in your power. It's for the good. It's helping a lot of folks. I hope you keep on doing it."

"I intend to," Hoby said. "But I can use all the help I can get."

"What I have to say wouldn't be of much help to you. If you want to find out, you'll have to decipher the contents of that paper. Or, better still, call that number and ask for Beaky. But you've got to discover it on your own. It might all be a bunch of wild-ass conjecture. Who knows?

"But you know Lamar," Hoby insisted. "Obviously better than most of us."

Harvey's face twisted into a sour grimace. "That's right. I know Lamar. And now you're going to have to get to know him better yourself."

34

Bob was entertaining the day shift with stories about his movie career. One of the workers, a Papago Indian, recognized him; too shy to say anything, he had a friend inquire if he was in fact Cowboy Bob Pringle. The workers at the Ajo plant were mainly Indians and Hispanics, in their forties and fifties; as youngsters, they'd spent a lot of time in movie houses. It was inevitable they would have seen Bob; back then, Bob's films appeared in every dirtbag movie house in rural America. The sight of Bob sitting at the counter strumming a guitar unleashed a string of memories in the Papago guy. The real past—a past full of hunger and prejudice and deprivation—disappeared like a froth of bubbles. Looking at Bob now, the Papago remembered the excitement of sitting in a cinderblock theater on a hard wooden bench watching black-and-white images flick across a bed sheet pinned to the wall.

"I think my favorite film, least the one I'm proudest of," Bob said, in response to a question, "was a film I did in 1940 called *Navajo Tears*."

Several men grunted and nodded. "I seen *Navajo Tears* ten times when it come out," the Papago declared.

"I still like that film best," Bob said. "And you know why? 'Cause it dealt honestly with a sorry chapter in our history."

"The Long Walk," said the Papago.

"That's correct. After Kit Carson smashed the Navajos at Canyon de Chelly in 1864, he rounded them up—men, women, children—and marched them across New Mexico to a pigsty near Fort Sumner known as the Bosque Redondo. Then, with little food and not much shelter, the Navajos were left to die on a bleak, salty, arid stretch of high plains, far from the canyons and glorious mesas of their ancestral lands. If you remember, I played a young cavalry officer sympathetic to the Navajos' plight. He shared his rations with the starving and became enraged when his commanding officer permitted the old men and women of the tribe to die like dogs in the rain and snow. He even fell in love with a Navajo beauty—you remember her? Played by Jane Bryam."

There were nods and murmurs of assent.

"The director was Fitzroy Brown. An Englishman, very proper. He didn't know much about the Old West, but he was sympathetic toward human suffering. He wanted to make a film that would remind people of what one race could do to another in the name of Manifest Destiny. He got ahold of a mediocre script and pumped large doses of action and human interest into it. Fortunately, there were also lots of kissing scenes between me and the beautiful Jane. He insisted on making the Indians' suffering as realistic as possible. At the end, he wanted me to tear off my insignia and gallop back to Canyon de Chelly with my lady friend and live happily ever after. But the producers knew that wouldn't wash. Instead, she dies— remember? And I get transferred back East to join Grant's army in Virginia, presumably to get myself killed in one of those gruesome Civil War battles. Hell of a movie. I'm proud to have been part of it."

"And after that, you started singing for a living," a voice called from the back of the café.

"That's right," Bob said with a rueful grin. "I thought it might be fun to be a real Hollywood cowpoke star."

"Don't feel bad, Bob. We still loved you. Soon as you stopped singing and got back on your horse, everything was okay again."

"Ain't that a bitch," Bob sighed. "You know, I don't know what happened to this country after the war, but all of a sudden nobody was willing to speak the truth or take chances anymore. It was like we started believing the propaganda we put out about ourselves to help us defeat the Japs and the Nazis. Everybody became more interested in behaving like a good American than in behaving like a good and truthful and decent human being. Anybody who spoke out was called a Commie. Everything became politicized. Normally generous and fun-loving people in the industry became grumpy and tight-assed. You couldn't make a film unless it was innocuous or contained the right message. It wasn't fun any longer. That's when they stuck me in those singing westerns. I want you to know how much I hated those goddamn singing westerns. I want you to know, too, that I won't go on television today and gush over how sweet and nice those westerns were and how proud I was to be teaching the kiddies good manners and the little girls to keep their knees together. Those films were terrible, and it helps me even now, thirty years after the fact, to confess that I did them for the money, that I did them so I could drive a fancy car and live in a big house. I'm ashamed of those movies—the fake fights, the idiot yodeling, the ridiculous gun battles. If I could burn them all up, right here and now in a big greasy bonfire, I'd do it."

"But look at all the pretty girls you got to kiss."

"That's true. But the taste of those lips in no way compensated for the amount of shit I had to eat along with it."

Harvey Phelps and Hoby Tibbs walked in at the end of this conversation.

"Ah, here's my pard," Bob said. "You ready to ride?"

Hoby nodded.

"Friends, I don't know if you know this gentleman," said Bob. "In practically all my movies I had a sidekick, and I am privileged now in my old age to be his."

"Ain't he the Ptomaine Kid?"

"In the flesh," said Bob. "The one and only. The man who single-handedly has been reclaiming bad hamburger for our stomachs."

"We're much obliged for what you did for Harvey," said one man. "We sure got tired of eating rabbit food."

Hoby waved his hand and nodded. "I'm glad I could be of help. You fellows like eating hamburgers?"

"Hell, yes!"

"I'm glad to hear that."

But his face was troubled and downcast, which Harriet questioned him about later when they were alone in the car, parked in a grove of cottonwoods a couple of hundred yards from the aluminum-sided building on the outskirts of Ajo that served as the airport terminal. "Bad news, huh?" she said, sitting close to him in the front seat of her battered Dodge Dart. A breeze crinkled the leaves of the cottonwoods.

"Kinda."

"You understand what's written on that paper?"

"Nope. But I've dedicated myself to finding out."

"Did Daddy really know Mr. Whammers?"

"He did indeed."

"Did he know him well?"

"I'd say well enough."

"Funny. I never heard him speak much about him."

"There's a lot about Mr. Whammers that your dad would like to forget."

"Is Mr. Whammers a bad man?"

"It appears so."

Harriet wrapped her arm around his shoulder. "I'm sorry you can't stay the night."

"I got to get back to work, Harriet. There's lots more hamburger out there that needs tending to."

Harriet's hair was short and frizzy. She had a round face, alert, expressive eyes, and a tight, voracious mouth. "Hoby, I know you think I'm a tramp . . ."

"What? Why would you say that?"

" . . . and I am, sort of. When I fall for a man, I fall hard and fast. And I fell for you like a paperweight through a basket of confetti."

"I don't think you're a tramp. You're passionate and you're truthful, and I like those things about you."

Hoby fixed his lips to her warm, moist cheek and let them linger there. "You're too smart for me, Harriet. I'm intimidated by smart women."

A flurry of quick pecks escalated into a passionate, full-tongued rooting. A moment later they fell out of the car into the dust, keeping the car between them and the terminal, heaving and groaning in the desert particles gyrating around them. Hoby with his trousers down around his ankles, Harriet with her skirt hiked up, the late afternoon sun blazing down upon the cottonwoods, shafts of light leaking between the crinkling leaves, dappling their naked flesh.

"God, Harriet, I can't believe this."

"I want you to do something," she wheezed.

"What?"

"I want you to bark."

"Huh?"

"Like a dog. I want you to bark and keep on barking."

"Jesus, Harriet."

"Bark, goddamn you!"

He barked and howled and snarled. His tongue swelled. With each thrust, his sore teeth quivered and throbbed. Hoby felt himself soaring up an invisible scale, the notes singing louder in his head. The final note was a doozy. It rang through his brain, blinding him, convulsing his tongue. With a bark that rattled the leaves, he gouged frantically a time or two more, then collapsed . . . spent, flabby, rimless, a deflated tire with no tread left to ride on.

35

The aviator-monk was sitting on the tarmac with his back to the wheel flap of the Savoia-Marchetti, enjoying the shade and the breeze that trickled over the runway, when Hoby and Harriet came up, holding hands, their clothes smeared with dust. He could tell they'd been spooning; their cheeks were the color of fried salmon. He waved listlessly. The heat was ferocious. He liked it better up there in the empyrean where the air was cooler, the view unobstructed. "Ready to go?" he called.

"Ready. Where's my pal?"

"Onboard."

"I hope I haven't delayed you."

"Not at all. I just got in from Yuma. It was hot in Yuma."

The aviator got to his feet. "The gin helped close your buddy's eyes."

"He needs the sleep but not the gin."

"I'll try and take off gentle as a bird so he's not disturbed."

"That's very thoughtful of you, Captain."

"I love my job, mister. Sitting here or at the controls, I dream of getting high and staying that way forever."

Eddie Winerick was polishing the gleaming handle to the fuselage door. "Find out anything interesting?" he asked Hoby.

"Too much. I don't think I care for that much information."

"It's not the information that hurts," said Eddie. "It's what you do with it that might."

"Right now, I'm too tired to care."

"You might consider looking a taurus in the eye," Eddie suggested.

Hoby looked down at him from the top step. "How come you know so much, Eddie? Where do you get your information?"

"I live alone on the edge of town. The door of my shack faces east to the place where the moon rises. At night, mockingbirds perch in the shrubs and confess their secrets. I've learned to understand their language."

"I envy you, Eddie."

"But I don't have a girlfriend, mister. Remember that. I never had a girlfriend in my life."

The pilot cranked the propellers. The aircraft trundled to the head of the runway. A man stepped out of the terminal and saluted. The pilot gave him the thumbs up and eased the throttles forward. The sweet bird bounced once, then twice, a third time before leaving the ground. Eddie and Harriet kept waving at the spot in the flawless blue sky long after the airplane disappeared into it.

36

Something inside Hoby snapped. For the first time in his life he was genuinely angry. He'd been angry before, in fits and spurts, but the effect faded quickly, the impact kicking up little more than the dust at his feet. His wife, to whom he was married for three years, used to complain that these fits mattered little more than a fart in a tin cup. She was fond of expressions like that; Hoby's passive, self-effacing personality brought out the best in her.

In those days, there was no limit to the amount of guff Hoby was willing to absorb. He wasn't interested in fulfilling his father's expectations of him; at the same time he stubbornly refused to formulate any of his own. He ran all over the Coachella Valley working at different jobs. "You ain't gonna find anything good to drink from that well," his wife declared the day he came home and announced that he'd given up grape picking to learn to fry hamburgers. She added cryptically: "You're trying to throw gravel in your father's face, but you'll only end up blinding yourself." Six months later she moved out of the house.

The statement, so mysterious when it was uttered, seemed perfectly comprehensible to him now. Hoby thought about it, and her, on the way back to Douglas. Bob was asleep, his lips blubbering like the oxygen unit on a fish tank. Anger was something he had shunted aside for most of his life. There was a lot about his father—his avarice, his stinginess, his shameless pandering to his social betters—that infuriated Hoby; but instead of voicing that anger, Hoby swallowed it whole, washing down the lump with copious swigs of alcohol. Soon as he began to seethe he got drunk, and instead of exploding, instead of confronting his father or whoever else it might be, he stifled the impulse with a bottle of sour mash.

But the beating the other night had caused something to crack. The fists that rained down on his face and shoulders triggered a long-suppressed rage, and, like a volcano after years of harmless rumbling, Hoby erupted with a fury. He replayed in his mind the memory of coming down with both feet on top of one of the assailants and hearing something crack under his boot heels. He replayed in his mind the scene where, with the concentration of a place kicker, he banged the toe of his boot against the other assailant's neck and felt the shock reverberate all the way to his hip.

37

It was dusk the following evening when he and Bob drove up to the truck stop ten miles west of Lordsburg, on the Arizona-New Mexico border. The job in Wilcox that morning had taken only a couple of hours. There was a WhammyBurger in Lordsburg and one farther east in Deming, but Hoby first had to pay a call at a truck stop at the base of the Peloncilo Mountains, on the edge of the vast, alkali plain that stretched east and south for twenty miles. Billy Stander's truck stop bought all its hamburger from L. G. Whammers. The meat was contaminated, and a call had gone out, loud and urgent, for Hoby's services.

The sun was just sliding behind the western peaks when he and Bob pulled up in the Buick. Livid pink and orange streaks flared across the sky. Hoby swung out of the car and started for the door of the truck stop, gimping along with a funny little limp, of which he took no notice but which Bob, trailing a pace or two behind, recognized immediately. It was his walk, perfected during the filming of *Fighting Fred Slade*—an awkward, off-balance shuffle that gave the impression of being uncoordinated and maybe even crippled. Scorned, shunned, despised, the Fred Slade of the film used the shuffle to fool his enemies into thinking he was not only stupid but physically inept. The disguise, thanks to a sympathetic script, had proven successful in several bar scenes. Bob was pleased that Hoby remembered it.

Hoby was wearing his holsters, and after sauntering up to the counter, he tucked his hands down into them. There were a few truckers at the tables, a half-dozen diners at the counter. As Hoby moved along, first a waitress then a couple of truckers fell silent, the waitress halting with a pot of coffee in her hand, the truckers pausing in mid-chew, forks poised halfway to their mouths. Then the place went silent . . . the truckers, the auto passengers, the two Norwegians hitching to New Orleans . . . one by one like jack-in-the-boxes they looked up at that end of the counter where stood the soft, plumpish, nondescript figure of Hobart Tibbs, a.k.a. the Ptomaine Kid.

Billy Stander peered through the slot notched in the kitchen wall.

"At fucking last," he sighed. His wiped his hands on his apron and sidled through the door.

Hoby drew his hands out of the holsters and pointed to the ceiling. "No handshakes, Mr. Stander," he announced. "My digits are too tender to be subjected to external pressure, no matter how gratefully applied."

"I understand, Kid, I understand. I'm just glad you're here. We're down to serving oatmeal and English muffins for supper."

"That's a dire predicament, Mr. Stander, dire indeed. This here's my partner, Cowboy Bob Pringle. You may remember him for the many movies he made back in the 1940s."

"Pleased to make your acquaintance," Billy said.

Hoby glanced around the kitchen. The situation was bad. Not only was the hamburger spoiled, but the cubed steaks had gone sour, the T-bones were festering, the link sausage Billy served with pancakes and eggs was turning green. The meat had been supplied to Billy direct from the WhammyBurger packing house in Deming.

Hoby let out a whistle of dismay. "How'd't get so bad, Mr. Stander?"

"It come on fast, Kid, without warning. One day last week, two of my help got sick. Then my customers started dropping like flies. It's not very comforting to watch people you've just fed upchuck all over your new linoleum floor. I don't know where it come from. It's like it's in the air."

Hoby drew his fingers out of the holsters and flexed them in the brittle kitchen light. The cooks and dishwashers stopped what they were doing. "This should be quite a challenge, Mr. Stander."

Billy gulped. "I'm ready to pay, Kid, whatever it costs. This roadhouse is my lifeblood. I built it with my own hands. When I die I plan to be buried out back."

"I understand, Mr. Stander. I'm prepared to do all I can to correct the situation."

He pirouetted on one heel in the soft glow of the recessed bulbs, holding his tingling fingers up to his face. His eyes gleamed like polished agates.

'All right, Mr. Stander, let's have it. Bring it all out of the fridge and dump it on the foor."

"The floor!"

"That's what I said."

Two men opened the refrigerator doors and pulled out everything they could find—patties, sirloin tips, filet mignons, T-bones, and chili meat hit the floor in front of the big griddle. "Mr. Stander, tell your customers that for the next three hours they can have nothing but coffee and sweet rolls."

"That's an awful long time."

"So's going out of business." He looked around. "Everyone stand out of my way . . ."

Hoby tramped around the stack of meat, muttering and growling and flexing his fingers. Once or twice he feinted toward the pile as if ready to charge, then pulled back with a grunt and a wag of the head. He was building up momentum, stoking a head of steam. Bob perched on a stool and plunked a background track with his guitar. After a minute or two of restless circling, Hoby gave a shout and dove headfirst onto the stack. Like a badger he began clawing a hole down to the floor. He attacked the steaks first—pressing, squeezing, gouging—followed by an all-out assault against the patties. Hunched over, he ground his thumbs across each patty, restacking them in piles of ten as he finished. The work was tedious, but Hoby had fallen into a trance and didn't seem to mind. The kitchen staff, the customers out in the serving area, everybody in the place looked on, enthralled. Bob thrummed a flurry of flamencan licks. The expression on Billy Stander's face was tense and spellbound.

Three hours later, it was over. Bob and Hoby, each clutching a six-pack of Corona beer, stepped out into the mild New Mexican night. It was exactly 10 p.m. The faint glow from the stars felt cool against Hoby's flushed cheeks. His hands ached, and he could barely crack open one of the cans and raise it to his lips. Bob drove, and as the Buick gathered speed along the interstate leading to Lordsburg, Hoby sank down into the seat.

"That was some performance," Bob remarked. "You been doing that since Yuma?"

"Oh, yeah. But tonight was something special."

"I'll say. You sure gave them their money's worth. I tell you, son, if your hands hold out, you'll have your twenty grand inside a week."

Hoby sloshed a foamy mouthful between his teeth. "It's like trying to swim up a waterfall. You know what I mean, Bob?"

"Don't know that I do."

"All the energy I can muster in my hands is never gonna be enough to cure all the sick hamburger lying around the Southwest."

"Maybe not. But you're doing something else that's even more important."

"What's that?"

"You're giving folks a sense of hope. You're making them believe that you can really make a difference."

"You can't eat hope, Bob," Hoby replied, finishing the beer and opening another.

"You'd be surprised. Let me tell you a story. I grew up in a tough lead-mining district near Joplin, Missouri, not far from a little town called Neosho. Back then the miners, at least those in southwest Missouri, weren't unionized, and the company that owned the mines where my pappy and his brothers worked treated them little better than a southern plantation owner treated his darkies. Well, one day a United Mine Workers (UMW) organizer came to Neosho to instruct us about the advantages of gathering ourselves into a union. Now we were just a bunch of Ozark hill people, dumb as whale shit, who all our lives—least my pappy and his brothers—had mined lead out of the earth for a paltry wage. We had heard about unions and knew they had gotten started up in the coalfields around Moberly but figured nobody had ever heard of us down in Joplin. The year, as I recollect, was around 1922 or '23. I was about ten or eleven.

"Well, this fella come down from Moberly. A plain-spoken fella, dressed the same as us, except his clothes were cleaner. He called us together in a little hall there on the main drag of Neosho, and he began to talk to us about the UMW and what a union could do for us. I still remember now, fifty years later, the expression of interest and concern that came over the faces of our people, especially my pappy and his brothers. Hope. That's what it was. Hope. The promise of something different, the chance to ease a few burdens, the possibility of living a better life. I remember my father coming out of that meeting with his fists clenched and his teeth flashing. It didn't matter that the company sent out a couple of bruisers to beat up the organizer and left him in a ditch with his skull cracked open. The union sent down another one and then another one until 1925 or thereabouts we had ourselves a first-rate organization the company finally had to negotiate with. At times during those years, it seemed as if we'd never win. The company was a hard-ass company, and they didn't want to cough up a penny more than they had to. But we hung in there. We persisted. We clung like dogs to the bone of hope that organizer threw to us, and we never let go. And goddamn if it didn't pay off. And goddamn if it didn't change our lives for the better."

Hobby waited before saying, "That's a nice story, Bob."

"Damn tootin' it is! I like the hell out of that story. It's helped me throughout my life during the good times and the bad."

Hoby fumbled for the paper, creased and folded in his shirt pocket. He shook it out in the glow of the dashboard lights, puzzling anew over the formulas and the outline of the state of New Mexico with Deming and Hatch and Las Cruces clearly marked, forming a distinct triangle. "I think when we get settled in Deming, it might be time to give Beaky a call."

"Good idea," said Bob. "You call Beaky and see if he can't help clear up the mystery for you."

38

Beaky refused to speak to him. All Hoby said was "This is the Ptomaine Kid" and bam! the receiver on the other end crashed down.

This was the following morning, around 9:30. Hoby went to work at the Lordsburg WhammyBurger. A curious place, designed in the shape of an Apollo spaceship; Lamar's nod, in the mid-1960s, to America's obsession with outer space. Only four of these structures had been built, all in New Mexico. The capsule rested on its base, conical nose pointing upward. The high ceiling made it difficult to air condition; the chronic overhead ate up profits. And now, with the spread of sick hamburger, there weren't any profits. The manager, a Vietnam vet with a prosthetic arm tipped with an old-fashioned hook, looked anxious and beleaguered as he recounted his woes to Hoby.

There was a message for him from Alfredo Reyes in Douglas: "Please call at your earliest convenience." Hoby did his business at the Lordsburg franchise in two hours, ate lunch, and went back to the motel. Bob was reading a William Eastlake novel. Hoby dialed the WhammyBurger in Douglas and asked for Reyes.

"Thank you for calling, Mr. Tibbs. I'm afraid I have some bad news."

"What is it?"

"It's back."

Hoby's stomach flopped like a spastic frog. "Oh, no."

"I'm afraid so."

"How bad?"

"It looks like the whole new shipment I got in yesterday afternoon. I ran tests on about sixty patties, and they were all sour."

"Did the meat come from Riverside?"

"This batch came directly from the packing plant in Deming."

"Son of a bitch."

"We've already had three calls. Last night some kids got sick and had to go to the hospital. The county health officer just called and asked me how I felt about closing my doors."

Alfredo's voice was tight and squeaky.

"Okay, Alfredo, okay. Tell the health officer you're not going to serve any more hamburger. I'll try and get back to you as soon as I can."

"The batch you fixed up was just fine, Mr. Tibbs. It's this new stuff that's causing the problem. Our damn competitors are trying to poison us."

"Let me make some phone calls, and I'll get back to you later today or in the morning."

"All right, Mr. Tibbs. Maybe you can do something. I saw those kids this morning in the hospital. They looked awful. They'll be okay, but the bacteria in this latest shipment is virulent."

Hoby hung up the phone.

"Bad news?" asked Bob.

Hoby told him.

"You better call Whammers and get a reading from him."

"That's just what I had in mind."

Lamar's secretary at the Riverside office, Mrs. Gatch, said Lamar was gone for the day and wouldn't be back until tomorrow afternoon. Hoby told her it was an emergency and that he had to get in touch with him fast. Mrs. Gatch said she'd leave him a message.

"You got his home number?" asked Bob.

"Unlisted. He never gives that one out, not even to me."

"What about this Manning fellow you've been grousing about?"

"He could be anywhere—Douglas, Wilcox, Benson. He should show up in a day or two."

"Wait for him."

"I'm too antsy, Bob. There's something going on somewhere, and I've got to find out where it is."

"The packing plant in Deming sounds like a good bet. That's a perfect place to foul up the goods."

"Sure, but if anyone's treating the meat there, they'll be able to cover it easily. That's a big plant, Bob. They see me waltz in wearing my holsters, and they'll draw the curtain down tight. To inspect that place properly'll take a battery of experts."

"Let me see that paper you got."

Hoby pulled it out of his shirt pocket and tossed it on the bed.

"Beaky didn't even say 'hi'?"

"When I told him what I wanted the phone came crashing down."

"What was the area code?"

"Same as here."

"Did the operator tell you what town the number was in?"

"She said it was Hatch. Or near Hatch."

"Hmm. Hand me the Rand McNally."

Bob opened the road atlas and spread it on the bed. "Hatch is on the Rio Grande. There's lots of irrigation there, which means there's lots of cultivation."

He stared at the paper, squinting hard at the formulas through his reading glasses. "Do your fingers tell you anything?"

"What?"

"Bring your hands over here and run them across this paper."

"C'mon, Bob. It's not a Ouija board."

"Look, my fingers aren't magical, and I know what they're telling me."

"What's that?"

"Go to Hatch. There's something in Hatch you need to see. Beaky lives in Hatch. You track down Beaky and lay a finger against his temple and tell him it's a snub-nosed .38 special. He's the guy you got to talk to."

"That's like finding a six-sided grain of sand on a beach!" Hoby protested.

"No, it isn't. You're out West, son. There's not as many people here, and those there are have a way of making themselves known when you need them."

"Sure, Bob, sure. All I have to do is go to Hatch and walk up and down the streets calling Beaky's name, and he'll appear."

"I'm surprised at you," Bob said, removing his glasses. "You been living in that damn Coachella Valley too long, with all those rich folks from the big cities. Your antennae has gotten messed up. People out here send and receive signals much easier. There's less in the way, less static in the air. Out here, when you want to get ahold of someone, you just send out a signal. Because of the lack of interference, the signal comes in loud and clear. Beaky knows you're gunning for him. He knows you're bound to find him. He knows he's eventually going to have to confront you."

Hoby threw up his hands. "How'd you get so smart, Bob?" he wondered.

"It's the gin, son. Gin does wonderful things to your brain. But you got to drink a lot of it, and you got to drink it every day."

39

They checked out of the motel and drove to Deming, sixty miles east on Interstate 10. The country was flat and arid, tufted with scrub cactus and patches of ugly brown grass. Halfway there, Bob said, "I saw your little friend this morning."

A chill inched up Hoby's spine. "What little friend?"

"The little fellow in the black trophy bag. I didn't peek inside the bag, son. I came out of the bathroom and there he was, sitting in the window staring at the open country. I thought it was an owl, but now I'm not too sure."

Hoby eased the Buick onto the shoulder and braked to a halt. He leaned back over the driver's seat, unzipped the bag, and lifted Otis out. He half expected the yellow orbs to fix him with an expression of reproach, but they passed over him as if he wasn't there. He propped Otis up between the guitar and the suitcase on the backseat and wheeled the car back onto the highway.

"Cute little critter," Bob said. "Where'd you find him?"

"I never told anybody, Bob. Nobody but me has ever seen him before."

"You don't have to tell me if you don't want to." Bob rinsed his mouth with a glug of gin.

Hoby drove another mile or two. Suddenly the story of his first encounter with Otis came tumbling out. He talked nonstop, telling Bob everything he could remember.

Bob peered over his left shoulder. From where it sat, the creature wasn't tall enough to see over the front seat or out the windows. Bob got the impression that the creature didn't really care about the car or anyone in it. He got the feeling that, despite the metal and chrome and black vinyl seats and engine parts, the creature was oblivious to the car. It was as if it had appeared in this world from a point way back in time, that it belonged to a totally different world than Hoby or Bob knew anything about. An ageless world with no beginning or end. Such an enigmatic creature . . . maybe it had consorted with the dinosaurs . . . maybe it carried within its memory images of the world as a vast, low-lying body of brackish water, wave-swirled by sluggish currents that ebbed and slowed to the ceaseless spin of the planet.

At Deming they turned north on State Highway 26. A few miles outside town they passed the packing plant. The WhammyBurger logo—a juicy patty squeezed between the layers of a tawny-colored bun—loomed over the gate. "Wonder what's in there?" Hoby muttered.

"Are your hands tingling?"

"Not yet."

40

Hatch didn't have a main street. The main street was the highway, which cut a wide curve through a motley cluster of shacks and adobe dwellings. The focal point was provided by a Texaco station, a grocery store, and a cantina. The distance between the signpost designating the name of the settlement and the bridge that crossed the Rio Grande east of town was barely a quarter of a mile. Someone had blistered the signpost with shotgun blasts.

Hoby guided the car to a halt in front of the cantina. Before getting out, he put Otis back into the trophy case. He parked in the shade, under a sycamore tree. Something compelled him to lock the car. There was nobody on the street other than a dog and a boy. The boy had a stick in his hand, and he whacked it against the scaly trunk of the sycamore. The dog lay in the dust, watching him. The boy didn't look up as the two Anglos piled out of the car. The stick occupied his attention. When it snapped, he continued to smack the tree with the stub.

The townspeople were Hispanics. In English and Spanish, Hoby asked questions in the Texaco station, the grocery store, and the cantina. No one had heard of Beaky.

In the cantina he flipped through the pages of the phone book. There were sixteen listings for Hatch, none of which matched the number on the piece of paper in his shirt pocket. On impulse, he called the number again and let it ring fifteen times before hanging up. Beaky had answered once before; how to get him to answer it again? He and Bob mulled it over as they sat at the bar in the dingy cantina, drinking a couple of bottles of amber-gold Popé beer.

The place was spooky, the patrons distant. The bartender was efficient, but after serving them he moved away to wash glasses. The dozen or more customers were *mestizo*, with a scattering of Anglo bikers dressed in leather tunics and tight leggings. They answered Hoby's inquiries with monosyllabic grunts. On the wall above the cash register, another Popé beer display was plainly visible, this one featuring a Spanish conquistador buried up to the neck in a pile of sand, with his eyelids peeled off and a swarm of red ants crawling over his face. The caption read: "Francisco Coronado Makes Amends for Having Destroyed the Zuni Pueblo in 1540."

"This beer has a funny taste," Bob whispered.

"I agree. Let's get out of here."

They bought a six-pack, and as the Buick rattled across the single-lane bridge spanning the Rio Grande, Bob spotted a dirt track leading down to the riverbank. "Let's slip down there and plunk our feet in the river," he suggested.

A few minutes later they were lying on the sandy bank, soaking their feet in the silty green water. At this spot, almost directly under the bridge, the river was no more than fifty feet from bank to bank. Behind them rose a bare, gritty dune; behind that, another, sturdier dune supporting a grove of willows and cottonwoods. A light breeze rattled the leaves. Clinging to the underside of the bridge was a colony of mud-daubed nests, built and inhabited by scores of bank swallows.

They lit up cigars and opened a couple of beers. In Lordsburg, Hoby had bought a Dahlgren switchblade with an oyster-shell handle. He liked the way the knife jumped in his hand when he pressed the button. He spiked the cigar with the tip of the blade and puffed out a cloud of smoke.

Otis was out of the trophy case, sitting in the sand next to Bob's guitar, the luminous orbs of his pale, owl-like eyes fixed on the bank across the river. A hedgerow of trees screened the town from view. Hoby was glad to be out of Hatch. If Beaky was there, they'd never find him. The town was well guarded.

"A man could do a lot of this and not get tired of it," Bob sighed, dribbling beer down his neck.

"You bet," Hoby sighed. "This is my idea of the afterlife."

A single-engine aircraft buzzed over the bridge maybe a hundred feet in the air. An old-fashioned biplane, with a yellow fuselage and wings and a loud, clattery engine.

Bob fell asleep, the cigar smoking between his fingers. Hoby reached over and flipped it into the river. With the other hand he stroked Otis's soft head. Then he fell asleep.

The biplane flew over again, lower this time, slanting past the trees on the far bank.

Bob awoke with a jolt, swatting at his jaw. Something had bitten him; a welt, hard and itchy, was already rising.

He looked around. The sun was practically in the same position in the western sky. He glanced at his watch; he'd been asleep for about fifteen minutes. Hoby was lying on his back, mouth ajar, snoozing, one hand curled protectively around Otis. Bob saw the eyes and shuddered. Round and gaping, the size of fity-cent pieces dipped in candle wax. He grunted and hauled himself up on his feet, his joints crackling. Just getting to his feet any more involved a major commitment. We die by increments, he decided, although presumably that was better than all at once.

He hobbled past the car, licking his dry lips, blood bubbling through his limbs. It felt good to stretch. He started up the narrow track cut into the embankment that hooked up with the road that slipped across the bridge. At the top he paused to catch his breath. The yellow biplane flew over a field behind the river, maybe a half-mile from where he stood, swooping low and fast like a swallow, making a terrific racket. Bright streams of fluid gushed from a dozen spouts trailing under the lower wing.

The biplane reached the end of the field, spun around in a tight loop, and zoomed back, depositing a sheen of iridescent droplets onto the stubby grass. Bob's hands clenched at his belt. His eyes widened. "That's it," he muttered.

Back down the bank he stumbled, his bare feet smacking the sand. Hoby was still asleep, his mouth gaping. "Kid, Kid," Bob gasped.

"Yo, Bob, what's up?"

"Something . . . over there . . . you oughta see."

"Sure, Bob. What is it?"

Hoby sat up, rubbing his eyes, staring down at his feet still bobbing in the muddy green water. "Must've fallen asleep," he said sheepishly.

"Come right now. Don't even put your boots on."

By the time they reached the top of the bank, the biplane had made another turn and was coasting over the field in the opposite direction, trailing a bright, bubbly veil.

"Do you see what I do?" Bob asked, breathless again after toiling up the embankment.

"Sure, Bob. It's a cropduster spraying a field."

"But do you see what's standing in that field?"

"Cattle. Lots of cattle. Lots of black-and-white cattle."

Hoby put his hands to his mouth in a prim, maidenly gesture. "You don't think . . . ?"

"Well, what does it look like to you?" Bob practically shouted.

"It looks like that airplane is dumping chemicals right on top of those cattle."

"Uh-huh. And onto the grass them cattle are munching right now."

"God . . . damn."

"And I bet the fellow that's flying that airplane is named Beaky."

41

The Buick idled on the side of the road, in the shade of a leafy willow. Bob and Hoby watched the biplane, waiting for it to finish. When the plane finally pulled away, gaining altitude and heading east, Hoby cranked the gearshift into drive and peeled onto the blacktop. The biplane cruised over Interstate 25, the main route between Albuquerque and El Paso. A minute later Bob and Hoby shot under the interstate, only to discover that the road they were on ended at a board fence bearing a sign that said

"Private Land. No Trespassers." There was no access to the interstate. They had arrived at the end of the asphalt. Behind and above them traffic whizzed by, heading north and south. Ahead a long, empty plain bunched up after a few miles into a series of drab brown ridges.

"Damn!"

"Don't let it stop you, son."

"We've run out of road!"

"There's plenty of land. Flat and level and easy. Hell, you could drive from here to Amarillo and not have to touch concrete."

"You think so?"

"You want to find out what this is all about, don't you?"

"You bet!"

"Then stomp the pedal and let's get going!"

The Buick tore around the barrier and roared across open country. Hoby kept his eyes on the terrain, while Bob kept tabs on the aircraft. The ground was rough and dry, with rocks stacked and scattered between clumps of sage and creosote. Over low mounds and down into shallow depressions the car hurtled, shock absorbers groaning, wheels skidding, kicking up clouds of dust and pebbles. They encountered a fair-sized wash, running east. Down into it they banged and rattled, the car nosing over a steep bank, then leveling out on the dry bed. So far it was easy going, the wash as smooth as a bulldozed strip.

"He's bound to hear us!" Hoby yelled. "He'll have landed and be waiting for us by the time we arrive!"

"Maybe not. Those things make a hell of a racket. I doubt if he can hear himself scream."

The wash crooked abruptly north, but instead of following it, Hoby went right up the side and over the rim and back onto the flat terrain, all four wheels clearing the ground, landing with a crash that rattled his teeth and made the frame groan. The wheels spun furiously across the hard-packed sand. "Sonuvabitch!" Hoby yelled.

"Bear down, boy! Keep bearing down!"

The biplane, glowing a bright taxi yellow, clattered over a foothill of the Caballo Mountains. Slowing the car, picking the way, Hoby skirted the ridge, avoiding a couple of rock outcroppings. A jackrabbit bounded into the brush. The Buick creaked audibly as Hoby worked it around the south end of the ridge and pulled into the mouth of yet another wide, easy wash. A steep ridge loomed ahead, a dry, barren escarpment plumed with yucca and prickly cactus.

Hoby's face was caked with sand and dust. "What now?" he gasped.

"He must've come down on the other side of that ridge."

"I think we can get around it in the car."

"And make enough clatter to wake up every snake in the county." Bob poked his head out the window. "See that defile winding up the ridge there?"

"Got it."

"I recommend we sneak up to the top and get a look at the land. Once there, we can form a plan."

"Shit, Bob, you're no mountain goat. That ridge must be five hundred feet high. I'll have trouble climbing it myself."

"Don't worry about me." He picked up the pint of gin and stuck it in his pocket. "You grab the canteen. Let's go."

Up they started, Hoby in the lead with the Dahlgren switchblade poking from his belt, Bob clutching the guitar. "What the hell you bringing that for?" Hoby panted.

"It saved your ass once. It might just save it again."

Up the narrow defile they went, climbing from rock to rock, breathing hard, clawing at the cracks and ledges. Every ten minutes they rested, holding their sides and wheezing, praying their hearts wouldn't give out. Sweat poured off Hoby's face. "Just my luck," he panted, "there'll be a goddamn rattler at the top wanting to play King on the Hill."

"Save your breath, boy."

It took almost an hour to reach the top. Behind them, to the west, the sun hovered over an inky blotch of mountains. Blowing, puffing, blood churning, they sprawled on their elbows and looked down into another valley, wider than the one they had just climbed out of. A strip of stony soil down the center had been graded over into a primitive landing site. The biplane was parked at one end, at the foot of the slope on which they rested. A hangar made of corrugated siding, open on three sides, stood next to the aircraft. Next to the hangar was a smaller structure, constructed from a mix of materials—rock, adobe, wood posts, metal sheets; a low, rounded hovel with a stovepipe chimney and a single wire running from a pole to another pole fifty feet away.

"There's your telephone," Bob whispered.

"You bet. Wish we had a gun."

"Damn things'll only get you hurt. We got to use our brains."

"I suggest we wait till the sun drops some more, then slip down."

"Maybe they'll invite us in for a drink," Bob retorted. "I figure there's got to be at least two, maybe three of them. Beaky's the bird we want, so here's what I figger we ought to do."

They waited another thirty minutes; when the shadows had filled nearly the entire length of the valley, they started down the slope. On their rumps, Bob holding the guitar so it wouldn't twang, Hoby flat on his back, feet up, like a kid riding a water chute. At the foot of the ridge, a few yards from the hovel, they got to their feet and went their separate ways. Crouched over, knife in hand, Hoby dashed toward the airplane. Bob crept around the back of the hovel. Pausing to make sure Hoby was in position, he stole up to the door, swinging the guitar over his head.

That was the signal. Hoby snapped the knife blade open. Just behind the spot where the wing was attached to the fuselage, just below the open cockpit, he plunged the point into the taut canvas covering the fuselage. "Hey, Beaky!" he called. "Get your ass out here! I need to talk to you!"

There was a commotion inside, the sound of a dish being dropped. A moment later a figure stepped out the door. A man, otherwise indistinguishable in the gloom blotting up the valley floor. "Who's that? Who the hell'er you?"

With both hands on the knife handle, Hoby marched from the wing to the tail section, tearing open a long, gaping rent in the fabric. "You hear that, Beaky? You know what I'm doing to your baby?"

"Get away from there!"

Beaky started forward, hobbling a few steps, then breaking into a quick, nervous run. At that instant another man charged out the door, hard on Beaky's heels. He hadn't gone more than two steps when there was a whoosh followed by a splintering crack as Bob's guitar slammed into his skull. The man went down. Beaky whirled. When he saw Bob advancing, he turned back and dashed the rest of the distance to the aircraft, pulling up short, nearly falling over his own feet, when he spotted the knife in Hoby's hand. Bob stomped closer, wagging the battered guitar. Hoby crouched down, snarling, his neck muscles bunched into tight knots, the knife in one hand, a rock in the other. Beaky's face went white.

"Okay, mister, okay! Take it easy! I'll tell you what you want to know. Only please don't hurt my airplane any more."

42

What Beaky told them was interesting but not that conclusive. Yes, for the past two months he'd been spraying the fields outside Hatch and another down by Las Cruces with a special kind of formula, brought to him in a milk truck by two men in matching bib overalls. Yes, Ralph Manning had been in touch with him by phone, telling him where to spray and how much. No, he'd never met Ralph, he'd only talked to him on the phone. Yes, he was aware that something peculiar was going on, but he wasn't a regular bonded cropduster, he was just a pilot and a damn good one, despite having only one eye (the other having been gouged out in a bar fight in Needles, California). No, he didn't remember the name of the chemical, although he did remember the type of bacterial poisoning the chemical induced in its victims. It sounded like the name of an Italian fish. Sal . . . salble . . . salmon . . . salmonella. That was it.

By this time the man on the ground had recovered, and he added a few details. His name was Howard. He was an aircraft mechanic. World War I-vintage biplanes were his specialty. He and Beaky came from Nebraska by way of Iowa, where, five years earlier, Beaky had lost his crop-dusting license when the biplane hit a utility pole and pancaked onto the roof of a barn, killing a Guernsey cow, a dozen chickens, and a cat. The two then moseyed out to Nebraska, crammed into the duster's tiny cockpit, but jobs were scarce there. Farmers were not inclined to put much trust in a one-eyed pilot. Down through western Kansas they went, working the odd job but with no steady prospects until one day in La Junta in southeastern Colorado, they were called on by two men in sharkskin suits. Glum, unsmiling men on a serious mission, who offered them a steady six-month spraying job for a cattle company in New Mexico. The location was in the boonies, but the pay was good and in cash to boot. All Beaky and Howard had to do was douse the location with chemicals three times a week.

"And mister," Beaky said, "I don't know who you are, and I don't know who they are. I just do my job and keep my ears shut. And for that, once a week me and Howard receive a stack of greenbacks from the sharkskin twins. I don't know if what I'm doing is right or wrong. I don't know what it's got to do with anyone or anything. I just do what I'm told, and I'm grateful for that."

Hoby was working on a steady upwelling of righteous anger that Bob could feel later that evening in the car as they motored back to Deming. "You just can't react, Kid," he warned with a shake of the finger. "You just can't let your rage get the best of you. You got to think and keep thinking. Who did this, and why? What can you do to stop it? What can you do to make sure it never happens again?"

"I know who did it, Bob. Ralph Manning and most likely Lamar Whammers. They been poisoning their own cattle, and when the cattle are slaughtered and made into patties, the meat is tainted. Their own meat, for Christ's sake! Why would anyone be so twisted to do something like that?"

Bob brushed his forefinger through the speckled mustache thatching his upper lip. "It's got to do with economics, Kid. My guess is that Beaky and Howard are little more than a couple of cogs in a big, complex machine. My guess is that if you draw back far enough and achieve a better perspective, you'll understand how all the cogs work together. M-O-N-E-Y., son. That's what it always spells out in the end."

43

They waited for Ralph in Deming a full day after Hoby had finished with the WhammyBurger there. Then they drove back to Lordsburg to inquire about him, but Ralph had already come and gone. There was the possibility that Ralph had contacted Beaky and that Beaky had told him about the surprise visit to the airstrip. But Beaky, realizing that if Ralph knew about the visit he would likely cancel all future spraying operations, had agreed with Hoby that he would keep his mouth shut until Hoby had a chance to collar Ralph and shake him down. Beaky and Howard got paid every Saturday. Bob and Hoby had made their raid on Wednesday. That meant Beaky would likely remain mum until Saturday, so he and Bob had three days in which to locate Ralph Manning.

They were coming out of a café in Lordsburg and had just reached the car when a shot cracked out and the window on the driver's side dissolved into a puddle of glass. Hoby fell on his face and rolled under the Buick. The shot came from a car cruising by on the busy downtown street, a compact Japanese model that picked up speed, tearing east out of town. "You okay?" Bob called from the other side of the car where he was crouched down by the wheel.

"Yeah . . . yeah. Who was that?"

"Like as not, our Douglas friends."

Hoby crawled out from under the car and stood up, legs shaking. "Did you see them drive off?"

"Yep. I think that can be classified as a warning shot. The next one will be meant for our heads."

Hoby couldn't control the shaking in his legs. He slumped down on the rear bumper, his face twitching.

"We better get out of here in case they circle back," Bob said. "Get around to the other side. I'll drive us out of here."

At a convenience store on the edge of town, Bob got them both a soft drink. He laced his with a slug of gin. Hoby took his straight.

"I was wondering when we'd hear from them," Bob said. "They're ticked about what we did to them in that alley in Douglas. We best look sharp now so we don't get bushwhacked."

Hoby's face was ashen. "I'm not made for this, Bob. I'm just an ordinary guy. I like to drink beer and pass out on a beach. Violence makes me sick."

"You expect to survive this horse opera, you're gonna have to get down low and hug the shadows and keep one person at all times between you and the street."

"That's you, Bob."

"Good old Bob. I knew the Lord had allowed me to live to a ripe old age for something. To be your flack vest. Shoot, boy, falling down a flight of steps is nothing compared to hanging out with you."

Hoby couldn't get a handle on what it meant to be mean and violent. Initially, he'd been delighted by the discovery of an untapped reservoir of righteous anger seething inside him. If he was going to survive in the hamburger world, he would need it. Maintaining it, however, required a measure of sheer nastiness he simply didn't possess. He had it, but only in fits and starts. Truth was, he didn't make a very convincing tough guy.

That night in a motel in Deming, Hoby worked up a disguise. Using a can of Kiwi cordovan shoe polish, he rubbed a glob into his hair, tingeing the curly black roots till they turned a garish orange. He decided to grow a mustache, and although he didn't have enough hair on his upper lip to fill it out, he intended to smudge in the gaps with an eyebrow pencil.

When he came out of the bathroom, Bob took one look and spit a mouthful of gin across the bed. "That's the worst-looking mess I've ever seen," he gasped. "That's not the way to do it. You look like a gumdrop."

"What should I do?"

"You got to blend in with the terrain, not stick out. You got to merge into your surroundings. You got to be able to move across the land without leaving a mark."

"I'm not a lizard, Bob."

"Well, you better learn to behave like one. Right now, you look like the kind of creepy guy who likes to feel up old women in a nursing home."

Hoby slunk back into the bathroom.

44

Las Cruces was the next stop. There were two franchises there, three in El Paso, one in Van Horn, Texas. As far as this tour was concerned, he was finished. He intended to get to them all, then speed back to California and confront Lamar. Despite what had happened, he still had a duty to perform; franchise managers were counting on him to show up. What happened after he completed the cycle was anybody's guess. His brain whirled like a spin dryer. His future as a hamburger healer was in jeopardy. So far, he had earned a chunk of dough, although how much exactly he had no idea. He had instructed the Riverside office to mail his checks to his house in Indio. The cash he had on hand was expense money, and he still had plenty left.

At the first WhammyBurger in Las Cruces they got a break. The manager told Hobby he was having dinner with Ralph that night in Mesilla, at a little restaurant on the square. They needed to talk business, but after that they intended to relax. Hoby was welcome to join them.

"I don't think so. I got to push on to El Paso. Lots of work to do tomorrow. What did you say the name of the restaurant was?"

Back at the motel, a Best Western near the junction of Interstates 10 and 25, Bob showed Hoby his latest guitar. A Gibson, with a mother-of-pearl inlaid ring around the sound hole, purchased in a pawnshop in Las Cruces.

"Too bad you never get to play it," Hoby remarked.

"Guitars," said Bob, his eyes lighting up, "were first used as weapons by Spanish minstrels in the fifteenth century, when Spain was occupied by the Moors. The Moors outlawed weapons among the Spaniards, so the Spaniards converted their guitars into weapons. The Moors had introduced the guitar into Europe during the eighth century. The Spanish figured out a way they could use it as both an instrument and a weapon. Where the soundboard goes they substituted oak or mahogany. They did the same for the sides. It muddied the resonance but made for a pretty durable slugging edge. A Moorish patrol, making the rounds in Grenada one night, paid no attention to the minstrels serenading their lady friends around a fountain. The next morning every member of the patrol was found with his head bashed in. The Moors never really caught on; in 1492, when they were finally driven out, the guitar was made the official instrument of Imperial Spain by Ferdinand and Isabella."

"Bob, we got to make some plans."

"I know, son, I know. I just thought you'd like to know that there's a historical precedent for knocking off bad guys with a stringed instrument."

45

Mesilla was on the outskirts of Las Cruces, an old Mexican town nestled alongside the Rio Grande, with a pleasant square ringed by a cobbled walk and lit with wrought-iron lamps. A church stood at one end; at the other, a bar and a gift shop. Along the sides of the square were bookstores, novelty shops, art galleries, and a restaurant called La Fonda. Plunk in the center of the square stood a gazebo built of pine boards, neatly trimmed and whitewashed. At 7:30, when Bob and Hoby pulled in, a mariachi band was blasting a medley of favorites to a mixed audience of locals, tourists, and dopesters.

Bob and Hoby took up their vigil in the Billy the Kid bar at one end of the square. They drank beer and waited. At 8:05, accompanied by the WhammyBurger manager and his wife, Ralph entered the square and walked through the front door of the La Fonda restaurant. Hoby recognized him immediately. An old-time thresher with scything blades churned across his stomach. They ordered more beer and waited.

At nine Bob strolled across the square. The mariachi players had disbanded, and the square was empty. Bob ambled into the restaurant, shook hands with the owner, and chatted with him for a few minutes. The owner asked him to sit down. Ralph and his party settled at a corner table. At 9:15, Bob excused himself and walked back across the square. Inside the Billy the Kid bar, Hoby fingered his Dahlgren switchblade. The blades of the thresher bit deeper into his stomach.

At 9:30, Bob and Hoby were sitting on a bench across from the restaurant. At 9:45, Ralph and his party came out, patting their stomachs and picking their teeth. As they crossed the street, heading for the gazebo, Bob and Hoby faded into the shadows. Ralph and his party shuffled on, chuckling and lighting up cigarettes. Ahead loomed the gazebo. Hoby slipped into view, his nose twitching like a rat's. "Hi, Ralph," he called softly.

Ralph gulped and started backpedaling, clawing at the night air. Bob halted his retreat by grinding the neck of his guitar into the small of Ralph's back. "I think you and the lady better go on," Bob said to the franchise manager. "Mr. Manning will be along presently."

The franchise manager looked concerned. Was that Hoby Tibbs looking so nasty and mean? He wanted to say something, but his wife was with them so he didn't say anything.

"Move along now," Hoby growled.

The expression on Hoby's face took the buzz off the three margaritas Ralph had enjoyed at dinner. "It's okay, Phil. I'll be all right. I know these fellas. They're associates of mine. I'll see you at the shop first thing tomorrow morning."

Hoby marveled at his cool. Inside, Ralph was a mess, but his face remained smooth and unruffled, the eyes behind the horn rims unblinking and clear. No doubt Ralph would protest his innocence. Hoby intended to make him confess something, if only his weight and age.

Hoby leaned his shoulder against the wall of the gazebo. A door creaked open. "In here, Ralph," he said. "I want it quiet and confidential."

Ralph couldn't make his feet go, so Bob gave him a helpful shove. Ralph was trembling. Chile relleno juice filled his mouth. Hoby knocked his legs out from under him and tumbled him to the floor. Then, knife in hand, he came down with his knees on Ralph's chest. "Ouf!" Ralph cried. The cry was followed by a squeal. Ralph's horn rims rolled into the dirt.

"I need to make this quick, so help me out," Hoby said in a clipped voice. "I met Beaky and Howard up in Hatch the other day. I saw the airplane, the chemicals, the cattle, the fields. What's going on, Ralph?"

Ralph kept his cool, his face as smooth and shiny as a pie plate. He'd never seen the point of a switchblade. Other than the tip of Lamar's finger, he'd never had anything pointed at him in anger.

"I . . . I don't know . . . anything," he protested.

Hoby tore open Ralph's belt and yanked down his trousers. At the same time, Bob jammed his knees against Ralph's shoulders and squeezed his head between his thighs.

"Your balls, Ralph. If you don't talk, I'll cut them off and feed them to the pigeons."

"Hoby . . . it's not what you think."

"Lamar engineered all this, didn't he?"

"It got . . . away from him. He didn't mean for it to go this far."

"Why, Ralph? Why would he poison his own hamburger?"

Tears bubbled up through Ralph's eyelashes.

"You tell me, Ralph. You tell me why or I'll dice your dick to tatters. I'm not the same guy you saw in Riverside. I been beat up, shot at, hoodwinked, and now I'm mad. I'm really mad, Ralph. I'm so mad I can't think. Don't push me. One little shove and I'm gone."

Ralph's mouth trembled. "Everybody's in on it, Hoby. All the chains. They all agreed to tamper with their hamburger to drive the price up. To make the public so desperate they'd pay anything. Then you came along . . . and Lamar sent you out on the road. The other companies thought Lamar had doublecrossed them. And Lamar did try and do just that. He had you on his side. What else could he do? If he didn't use you to clean up his hamburger, some other company would. So I was instructed to follow behind and make sure every new shipment that came in after you left was also tainted. We had to go along with the others. We all agreed that for six months we would make the hamburger inedible. Then we would announce that it was all cured and start serving again, only at a higher price. By then people would be so starved for hamburger they would pay anything. By the end of the year we'd have made up the lost profit."

"Lousy . . . rotten . . . motherfuckers."

"It's not all Lamar's fault," Ralph insisted.

"The hell it's not."

"It got out of hand. There were other factors involved."

"The only factor I know was his greed and your greed and the greed of all the other hamburger hogs."

"Hoby, if you pitch in with us, it'll be better for everyone. There's plenty for all of us. We're talking millions here."

Hoby's face flushed with rage. "You're asking me to do what?" he roared, so loudly that Bob waved a finger in his face to get him to tone it down. "You scumsucker! You stinking bastard!"

But he couldn't bring himself to retaliate. That kind of violence just wasn't a part of his make-up. He lowered the knife and rolled off Ralph's chest. "I got a job to do, Ralph, and I intend to do it. But when I get back to California, I'm gonna spill and spill big. This news will make headlines in every newspaper in America, and your name will be right at the top. When I get through with you, Ralph, you won't be able to get a job picking scabs off dead winos."

46

Hoby kept his promise. The next day in El Paso he started in on the first of the three WhammyBurger franchises. The effort was futile. He knew that as soon as he walked out the door the meat would turn sour, but the job was there, and he was the only one who could do it. The tingling sensation in his fingertips had diminished. To get through the job, he had to remind himself that what he was doing was really worthwhile.

That first night in El Paso—weary, his muscles aching—he stood with Bob in the Acme Saloon on San Antonio Street sipping a tequila sour. A plaque on the wall reminded them that they were treading hallowed ground:

> On this spot in August 1895, John Wesley
> Hardin, the notorious desperado, was
> shot and killed by John Selman.

Hoby's scalp prickled. By all accounts, Hardin had been bushwhacked while standing at the bar throwing dice with a friend. "The bullet entered the base of the skull posteriorly and came out at the upper corner of the left eye," the coroner wrote.

Hoby turned back to face the door. It was through that door that John Selman had emerged, seeking retribution for a slight Hardin had (supposedly) directed against his son. The denouement was no classic western shootout, the sort that Cowboy Bob had enacted in grade-B flicks. Reportedly, Selman didn't call out Hardin's name or give him a chance to draw. He slipped through the door, gun in hand, hammer cocked, and fired. "Four sixes to beat," John Wesley said to his friend, handing him the dice. And then he died.

Hoby's scalp crackled. The bullet crashed through his consciousness, fouling the taste of the tequila. His shoulders knotted up under his ears. "I really don't like this," he muttered to Bob. "It's as if I can feel the muzzle of a .44 nudging between my shoulder blades."

Bob laid a hand on his wrist. "The two guys that tried to drill us in Lordsburg," he said. "They could be here."

Hoby glanced around the room. The air was smoky, the tables packed with rowdy men and women having a good time. "How can we know?"

"We can't. Until we see their faces, we won't know."

"My shoulders are killing me, Bob. My blood pressure must be at stroke level."

"Terrible, ain't it?"

"We got to find those two guys."

"Then what?"

"Shoot them. Shoot them before they shoot us."

"Someone will take their place," Bob sighed. "There's always another one out there to dog your steps."

He drained the last drops in his glass. "You need to learn to unwind, son."

"I feel like I'm going to implode. I can hear the fuse crackling up my spine."

Loud voices dinned against their ears. Harsh, strident voices, full of bluff and swagger. There, at his feet, crumpled up like a paper bag, John Wesley Hardin lay on the floor in a pool of blood. Another bad guy avenged. Hoby leaned down to touch the cold, dead face.

Bob squeezed his elbow. "Come with me," he said.

47

Bob drove the Buick to a nightclub/brothel located a few blocks from the Rio Grande. Los Corrales, it was called, a half-dozen single-story stucco buildings with carved wooden doors and red-tiled roofs, situated on ten acres of prime property just east of downtown El Paso. A venerable hostelry, built in the nineteen teens on what was then the edge of town. Over the years the city had grown around it, cutting it off, stranding it high and dry. The owners took what measures they could to insulate the grounds from unwanted encroachments. In 1960, a screen of oleander shrubs was planted around the perimeter. In 1967, a high-wire fence went up. As the city grew and expanded, the old places, those with a bona fide connection to the past, the atmospheric joints, were blotted up by new buildings. To preserve what was left of the original Los Corrales, in 1973 the management permitted entry by invitation only. No electronic contrivances were allowed. Music was provided by live bands. Within this cloistered space the air, unlike the air in the city proper, smelled fragrant and sweet. Countless plants and flowers bloomed on the grounds. Traffic noises were screened to a hum. Inside, guests lounged, strolled across manicured lawns, played badminton and croquet. They relaxed in the pool. They jigged to live music. They drank, smoked hashish, and fornicated.

Hoby had never seen so many good-looking women in one place. Black women, white women, brown women, red women, yellow women. They were everywhere. They outnumbered the men two to one. They stood at the bar, dined at the tables, played in the pool, swatted shuttlecocks back and forth, cavorted and danced. They touched and talked and laughed with warmth and affection. When a man approached—any man, even the most tentative and uncertain—they held out their arms and welcomed him. It wasn't a place for swaggering macho types. There were few conquests to be made, few battlements to assault. The women preferred thoughtful, friendly types, eager to share and give something in return, eager to offer comfort and understanding, eager to disburden themselves of the weight of their concerns.

Some men came just for that. Some came not to have intercourse or to be fellated but to be stroked and coddled. In private rooms, the women stripped the men and wrapped them in terrycloth breechclouts. They rubbed oils on their bodies and powdered their crotches. They crooned in their ears and hummed on their testicles. They buffed their toes and fingered their nipples. Orgasm was part of the experience but not the exclusive focus. The main idea was relaxation . . . deep, easy, slumbrous relinquishment of the nerves and corpuscles to a condition of near-perfect bliss.

"Where'd you find this place?" Hoby asked as he and Bob stood at the bar.

"It's the best-kept secret in America," Bob declared. He was wearing a sequined vest, a rhinestone belt, Dan Post boots with alligator toes. His white hair was fluffed into a pompador. His blue eyes gleamed with anticipation.

"Tonight's the night, eh?"

"I have an erection," Bob said proudly. "Well, I don't have one yet, but I will soon. At my age, it doesn't just appear. It has to be summoned."

"And these, I presume, are the ladies who will beat the tom-toms?"

"They've never failed yet."

The owner was an old pal of Bob's, a former film director for Republic Studios named Bud Hospeth. He greeted Bob with a hug and shook hands warmly with Hoby. He was a small-statured man with a bony, jovial, bug-eyed face. He wore a beret and an ascot, around his waist a tasseled sash. He looked like an ersatz Turkish pasha right off a Hollywood set. He smoked Balkan ovals in a tortoise-shell cigarette holder, clamped between his teeth at a jaunty angle. He talked out the side of his mouth in a tumble of words, punctuated by an occasional bubble of saliva. Anything they wanted, liquid or of the flesh, Bud said was on the house. Bob ordered a gin and tonic. Called to the phone, Bud excused himself and disappeared into his office. Later, when Bob was out on the floor foxtrotting with a nubile Asian woman, Bud came up to Hobby. "Enjoying yourself, Mr. Tibbs?" he inquired.

"Very much. This place is incredible."

"A hard-on is not the only prerequisite for having a good time," Bud observed. "I was stationed in Ankara with an intelligence unit during the Big War and I learned a great deal about the art of pleasuring the other parts of the body."

"The women are magnificent."

"They are, aren't they? They come here to relax and have fun. They come here to please themselves and to learn how to please others. They come here voluntarily, because they want to experience something they can't experience anywhere else."

"What's your policy regarding bad guys?" Hoby said with a twinge.

"Oh, we get one or two every now and then. They don't last long. We've some bruisers who patrol the grounds, although it's usually the women who police the area best. If a guy gets rough or abusive, they all pile on and kick the shit out of him. Don't laugh. I've seen it happen many a time. These ladies are not to be trifled with. They don't come here because they're down and out and need to be smacked around to feel wanted. They're stubborn and independent and proud. They know what loving is all about. They're here to love and be loved—to talk, listen, comfort, soothe, and be comforted in return. Those who prefer being caned or strapped or whipped need to move on down the street. This is a place for tender caresses and childish intimacies. It's a place for laughter and surrender."

"Bob looks like he's having a good time."

"Bob's a prince. Prince Bob Pringle, the last of the true cowboy royalty," Bud declared, snorting cigarette smoke between his teeth. "Did you know that back in 1947, when he was at the top of his game, Bob used to share his salary with the gaffers and the wranglers? Bob Pringle, the Wobbly Cowboy. Oh, they tried to bill him differently and make him into a yodeling asshole, but the identity never really fit. The one name all his colleagues knew him by was the Wobbly Cowboy. The man was a socialist in the best sense of the word. He believed in sharing. He believed in ridding the world of economic inequities so people would have a better chance to live up to their potential. What a guy. What a champion. In 1968 he floated me a fat loan so I could buy this place. He's a brick. A solid, gold-plated, gold-veined brick. I love him. He cares about people. He doesn't like to see them suffer. He offers advice. He offers hope. If we had five more like him, we could change the world."

Later, Hoby was on the dance floor, snuggling a Junoesque beauty from Clovis, New Mexico. They were swaying, hugging when Bob trotted up, clutching the hand of a sparkly redhead.

"This is great, Bob."

"Glad you like it."

"I think I'm in love."

"That's the way it ought to be."

The four of them danced together for a little while, laughing uproariously.

"Kid," Bob wheezed. "I think I'll be retiring soon."

"The summons worked?"

"Yep. I best take advantage of it."

"Sweet dreams, Bob."

"You kids don't stay on your feet too long."

Hoby had no idea what time it was when he fell into bed. He was frazzled but full of pep. He rolled around with Clovis, whinnying with delight. Clovis went to work on the tightness in his chest and thighs. Under her prodding tongue, the tightness eased and he found himself floating like a lily pad on the surface of an unblemished pond.

48

The next afternoon he said goodbye to Bob. They were standing at the foot of the International Bridge between Juarez and El Paso. Bob carried a duffel on a sling around his shoulder. In his hand he held the new guitar. The air over the Rio Grande was gritty with fumes. In the western sky, slotted between the smokestacks of a coal-converting plant, the sun looked as pale as a lemon drop.

"I wish we didn't have to do this," Hoby said.

"It's warming up," Bob replied. "I got to get down to Durango. A friend in Juarez has offered to drive me. I can hardly wait to bury my nose in a bed of pine needles."

"It won't be the same without you, Bob."

"Well, son, you know what a cowboy's life is like. Even a couple of faux cowboys like me and you."

"It's damn lonely, that's what it is," Hoby said in a husky voice.

"You be coming to Douglas in October? I plan to be there then."

"Bob, I'd crawl on my belly across a field of mating armadillos to ride with you again."

Bob adjusted his hat, squaring it low over his eyes. "All the best then. And try not to take this hamburger thing too seriously."

"Can't help it, Bob. It's my life."

"It don't have to be."

"I'm too dumb to know any better. I think I was born to save the world. This little piece of it at least."

"Sometimes to save the world you got to turn away from it."

"I don't understand that, Bob."

"Someday you will. You're a good man, Hoby Tibbs. You deserve a better fate than to squander your energies dealing with the likes of Whammers and Ralph Manning."

"What do you suggest?"

"Oh, it'll come to you. I suspect it's already inside your head. It just hasn't clicked yet."

"Think so?"

"Sure. You just have to make up your mind that you're tired of being a target. That you don't care anymore to be caught in anybody's crosshairs."

Hoby nodded gravely. "I'll try and learn that, Bob."

"Watch the lizards, son. They can teach you a lot."

He swung the guitar under his arm. "Well, I best be going. If you're around Douglas next fall, look me up. I'll be staying at the Hotel Gadsden. So long, Kid."

"So long, Bob."

Hoby took his hand and squeezed it hard. "I'll miss you."

"I'll miss you too, son. We had some great adventures together."

Hoby couldn't keep back the tears. He promised himself he'd be strong and not make a scene, but now that the moment was upon him, his resolve turned to mush.

Bob swung an arm around his neck and pulled him close and kissed him on the cheek. "Never done that to a man before," he said sheepishly. "I better get goin'. So long, Kid."

He turned and started over the bridge. At the halfway point he paused and waved, but Hoby could barely distinguish him from the other figures hurrying back and forth. For a long time after Bob dropped out of sight, he stood there on the El Paso side, crying his eyes out.

49

Van Horn, southeast of El Paso—the final stop on Hoby's tour—was located on a high plateau surrounded by solitary peaks and ranges, separated by miles of open country. A rectangular plaza provided the focal point, and it was here, in traditional Latino fashion, that the townspeople gathered in the evenings. While the young men stormed up and down Alvarado Street in their automobiles and motorcycles, the old people gathered in the plaza to talk and play cards and dominoes.

In El Paso, the particles from industry and automobiles clogged the air and snagged the nasal passages. Breathing was a chore in El Paso but not in Van Horn. In Van Horn the air was crystalline.

The franchise was easy. There wasn't much hamburger on hand because there wasn't much demand for it, and Hoby soon purged the little there was of microbes. By mid-afternoon the patties were glowing with health, ready to sizzle on the grill. It was the least demanding job he'd had since Yuma. The proprietors, Avery and Constance MacKenzie, seemed disgruntled. Theirs was the only hamburger stall in town, and they should have been ecstatic. But they weren't. All the time Hoby was there, they groused and complained. It appeared that few people in Van Horn actually ate hamburgers.

"How come?" Hoby wondered. He had finished treating the meat and was sipping a soft drink.

"They'd rather eat beans," said Constance, wrinkling her nose in disgust.

"Beans? What kind of beans?"

"All kindsa beans, but mainly pinto beans."

"Back where we come from in Alabama not even the colored people ate that many beans," Avery growled.

"What's wrong with beans?"

"It ain't American," Avery said. "Goats eat beans. Squirrels and rabbits eat beans. Apaches eat beans. But white folks ought to eat hamburger. It's what their digestive tracks are adapted for."

"Problem is," said Constance, her eyes widening, her voice lowering to a whisper, "there ain't that many white people in this town."

"Mexicans," Avery commented.

"But no niggers," said Constance.

"Nope, they's one nigger family," Avery corrected. "The Bateses."

"He's a white nigger," said Constance.

"Why's that?" asked Hoby.

"'Cause he loves hamburger!" Avery shouted. "You ought to see that boy put them away! Damned if he ain't my best customer. Without him, I'd go broke!"

"I think we're about to go broke anyway," said Constance. "Van Horn is no place for a hamburger enterprise."

"Beans," Avery growled, curling his lips. "All these folks care about is beans."

"Now what do you think of that, Mr. Ptomaine Kid?" Constance barked.

"I don't know."

"Well, I do," Avery grumped. "It's not American. No place where people eat that many beans belongs on this side of the Rio Grande. It goes against the grain of what we believe ourselves to be."

Beans, or whatever it was they ate, made the townspeople look healthy. Their flesh glowed, their hair was thick and glossy, they walked with a vigorous step. The interplay, especially between the old people, was lively and alert. They shouted, laughed, and touched.

Hoby ate dinner in a café on the rustic plaza. The fare was simple: cornbread, rice, green salad with black olives and goat cheese, beans flavored with salsa. Hoby chewed the beans slowly. A pungent odor crept into his nostrils. Figures of animals, drawn with crude vigor, adorned the café walls: pumas, antelope, coyotes, rabbits. The figures were colored with bright oils. They weren't faithful depictions but rather spiritual renderings of the essence of these animals.

Hoby finished the beans and sipped ice tea. Outside, it was nearly dark. A glabrous yellow moon rose over the cottonwoods shading the plaza. Hoby settled himself on a bench. Close by, on another bench, sat a *viejo* with a wrinkled face, dressed in a dark suit and white shirt. The shirt was buttoned at the collar with a gold stud. The knob of a mesquite cane poked between his gnarled fingers. The man nodded politely. His eyes, staring out from the cracked vellum of his face, were like tiny pinspots, his features refined and delicate.

"And how are you this evening, *señor*?"

The voice was old, high pitched, piping in the upper registers, distinct, sharp.

"Very well, thank you."

"You are enjoying our fine country air, perhaps? Van Horn is famous for its air."

"The air is delicious. I've been here half a day and already I feel better."

"The air is fresh here, *señor*. The mountaintops are covered with pine trees, which give off a resinous scent. Down here, on the plateau, the sun warms the earth and makes it rise like the crust on a loaf of bread. At night, when the cooling winds blow, the crust settles into place."

Hoby offered the man a Joya de Nicaragua, and when the man accepted and pointed to the spot beside him on the bench, Hoby shifted places. The man dug into his coat pocket and pulled out two wooden matches, and together they ignited their cigars and examined the tips to make sure they were lit all the way around.

"I wonder, sir, if I may ask you a question," Hoby began. "I am a stranger here, and a few things about this place puzzle me."

"*Señor*, you may ask me anything you wish."

"Well, sir, I'm in the hamburger business. I travel from town to town, curing bad hamburger meat. And I notice in Van Horn that there's only one hamburger stand, and it isn't very popular. I wonder if you could explain this to me."

The man looked up at the full-bodied moon rising over the silent trees. He puffed on the cigar. "The people here, *señor*, do not like hamburger meat. They eat little meat of any kind. It is difficult for them to digest, and it makes them sluggish. The people of Van Horn, *señor*, do not like to feel sluggish. Tired, yes, but not sluggish."

"But hamburger can be nourishing."

"Perhaps so to your taste, but not to ours. We are a bean people, *señor*. We live close to the earth. We like the plants and berries and tubers that grow in the ground. Certainly we eat meat—quail, rabbit, dove, deer from the mountains. But in hamburger we have little interest."

"Why is that?"

"We do not like to eat meat that has been artificially prepared. We do not like to eat meat that has been raised to be slaughtered for our table. There is no magic in that. There is no ceremony. The cow does not try and escape, and we are not permitted the adventure of chasing it down. Also, we are not called upon to ask its permission to kill it. Do you ask a cow fattening in a pen whether you might have permission to kill it? Of course not. The cow would not understand. She would gape at you with her big dumb eyes as if to say, 'Why are you asking me this? You created me for the purpose of eating my flesh. Don't talk to me of permission or rituals. Take my life, and take it quickly and painlessly. That is the least you can do for me.'"

"Your beans are very tasty," Hoby said.

"The bean, *señor*, is the nugget of the earth. It contains all the earth's minerals and all the earth's vitamins. If you treat the earth with consideration, she will give you back your life in the form of a bean. It is a cycle, an exchange."

"I guess I never thought of the bean that way."

The old man chuckled and made a mark on the ground with the point of his mesquite stick. "Many people, although they eat beans every day, never learn this. As you eat the bean, you must listen carefully to the stories it tells. The bean tells the oldest stories of all. It tells you stories that go all the way back to the beginning of time."

They finished their cigars in silence. The moon rose like a pumpkin over the trees. A mockingbird whistled and sang. Hoby smoked the cigar down to a nib and dropped it in the dust. He stood up and with a formal bow took leave of the old man.

In his room, he drew back the curtains and opened the window. A powdery light dusted the floor. He took Otis out of the trophy case. He settled on the bed and put his ear to the feathery chest. The heart went tung tung tung . . . evenly spaced beats, resonant as a timpani. Hoby missed Bob, but at least he had Otis. He missed Harriet, but at least he could be with Otis. The creature's eerie yellow eyes stared past him out the window at the moonlit streets.

Hoby cradled Otis in his arm and leaned back against the pillows and stared out the window. The moon gilded the street with a warm liquid glow. Few cars passed. Hoby breathed slowly; his eyelids drooped. He was awake—his eyes were open—but he couldn't feel any part of his body. The only weight he could feel from his scalp to his toes was the weight of the thought of how blissful it was to be weightless.

That night he dreamed of beans.

50

Hoby hurried back to Indio with one word sizzling in his brain: Lamar. Find Lamar and get the story from him. Track down Lamar and confirm Ralph's story. Get all of the story from Lamar: the idea behind the conspiracy, the actual plan, its implementation, Hoby's inadvertent presence on the scene. Once he located Lamar, Hoby knew he could get him to talk. Right now Lamar wasn't answering any phone calls, but that wasn't surprising. No doubt he was thinking up what to tell Hoby. And the newspapers. And the television stations. Because once Hoby confronted Lamar, he was going straight to the media. But before he coughed up his side of the story, he wanted a confession from Lamar. In person, face-to-face. Lamar owed him that much.

By driving sixteen hours and not stopping in Ajo to see Harriet, he made it back to Indio the following night. It was nearly dark when he steered the reliable old Buick down the narrow lane between the rows of date palms. He braked to a halt in front of the duplex and shoved open the door. Tulio had seen the headlights bobbing down the lane and stepped out to investigate. When he saw Hoby climb stiffly out of the car, he gave a shout and leaped off the steps. "How was it, man?" he cried.

"Long," Hoby replied through cracked and peeling lips. "Long and difficult."

Tulio helped carry in his gear. Hoby brought the trophy case in first and put it down on the bedside table. Under the bright kitchen bulb, Tulio saw him clearly. Hoby looked tired, but there was something else about him. His face, normally so open and receptive, seemed troubled. The features, especially the eyebrows, were pinched together in a brooding scowl.

"You okay, man?" Tulio asked, after they settled in the chairs outside on the lawn with a beer.

"Tired, Tulio. I'm really tired."

"Everything go okay?"

"Sure . . . sure. I got to all the places I was supposed to go. I did exactly what was required of me."

"You don't sound too happy about it."

"I think I worked too hard. I had some extra duties that popped up unexpectedly."

"I have something to tell you, man . . . "

"What is it, Tulio?"

"I have some bad news for you. For us."

"Let's have it."

"The widow . . . she going to sell this place."

"That is bad news."

"I found out for sure two days ago. I got a letter from her lawyer telling the details. A developer from San Bernardino is buying it. He going to level all the trees and put in twenty-five units. Condominiums for middle-income people. We got two months to get the hell out. They bring in the dozers September 15."

The beer slipped from Hoby's fingers and overturned on the porch floor.

"You got to try and talk to her, man."

"And say what? If her mind's made up, her mind's made up."

"You're a celebrity, man. She know who you are. The whole valley knows who you are."

"Ah, Tulio . . ."

"She admires what you been doing. Maybe you could go visit her and get her to change her mind. Maybe you could find out if she got another orchard she like to rent out. She a rich lady, man! She got orchards all over this valley."

"Oh, Tulio . . ."

"I'm sorry, man. I know you're bushed."

"What're we going to do?"

"I don't know. You got to see the widow. You got to at least get her to hear our complaints."

"I can't do it tomorrow. I have to go to Riverside. That will take the day."

"Next day then. Maybe you can call her tomorrow night and make an appointment."

Where am I going to get the strength for all this? Hoby wondered.

"Your dad called. He been calling about fifty times, wondering when you be back."

"How did he sound?"

"Okay. Drunk a little, but friendly. He say he got a better idea to invest your money than a hamburger shop in Indio."

"Oh boy," Hoby muttered.

51

The next morning he was up and on the road to Riverside by eight. Lamar considered the morning the optimum time to get things done. If he was coming in that early, Hoby wanted to surprise him. If he wasn't coming in, Hoby intended to rattle the walls until he found out where he was hiding.

The receptionist in the lobby of the WhammyBurger building greeted him politely. He gave his name, but she didn't show any special enthusiasm. Hoby expected to be sent right up, but instead she buzzed Lamar's secretary, Mrs. Gatch, on the third floor. The receptionist told the secretary that a Mr. Tibbs was waiting in the lobby and would like to see Mr. Whammers. The secretary told the receptionist to tell Mr. Tibbs that Mr. Whammers was out of town and wouldn't be back until Monday.

Hoby seethed. "Then where is he?" he asked in a loud voice.

The receptionist asked the secretary, who told the receptionist to tell Mr. Tibbs that she was sorry but that information was confidential and there was nothing she could do.

"Do you know who I am?" Hoby boomed.

"I'm sorry, Mr. Tibbs, but those are Mr. Whammers's personal instructions," said the receptionist.

Hoby stormed away from the desk and started up the stairs.

"Mr. Tibbs!" cried the receptionist. "Come back here! You can't go above the ground floor without authorization!"

By the time he reached the second floor, Hoby thought he heard a bell ringing somewhere on the premises. On the third-floor landing, blowing and panting, he yanked open the fire door and stalked down the hallway. The door to Lamar's office was locked. Through the glass pane he saw Mrs. Gatch stand up from her desk with a sheaf of papers in her hand and start for the door of the inner office. He banged on the glass. She looked up, saw his face, and stepped into the inner office, closing the door behind her. Hoby slugged the glass and kicked the door. Two corpulent guards, bellies spilling over their belts, converged on him from opposite directions. They wore blue uniforms with fancy insignia and black leather belts from which dangled an arsenal of revolvers, billy clubs, flashlights, handcuffs, two-way radios, and Mace cans. "That's enough of that," warned Guard Number One, drawing his billy from the loop.

"Where the hell is Whammers?" Hoby shouted.

"I think you better come with us," said Guard Number Two.

"Do you know who I am?"

"Sorry, Mr. Tibbs. Mr. Whammers is gone for the weekend. He won't be back till Monday."

"I've got to see him!"

"You want to come nicely, or do we have to drag you?"

In the elevator, Hoby struggled to contain his fury. "You guys are screwed, you know that? I got information about Lamar that'll blow the lid right off this building. You like your job, don't you? Well, you can start looking through the want-ads tonight, 'cause next week you'll be out on the street."

"This way, Mr. Tibbs." With a burly man on either side gripping his elbow, he was guided through the lobby, past the scowling receptionist, out the front door.

52

He sat in his car for thirty minutes, smoking and banging his foot against the dashboard. Fuming, seething, smoldering. Finally he calmed down enough to consider what he ought to do. If he could get to the third floor without being seen, he was confident he could extract the relevent information from Lamar's secretary. Mrs. Gatch was a mean old bitch; she'd been Lamar's secretary for fifteen years. Surely the pressure of the switchblade against her throat would make her squawk. He remembered there was a back door to the building; the day of the press conference he'd come in that way. He slipped the knife into his pocket.

The building was a drab, four-story affair located on the fringe of a busy residential district a few blocks from downtown Riverside, California.

Other than the WhammyBurger logo over the front entryway, it had no distinguishing features. Lamar's taste in office-building architecture was bland and functional. The place looked tawdry—too much mortar, too much white plaster; the windows were pinched and tiny. Lamar and his staff occupied the offices on the third floor. The other floors were tenanted by an accounting firm and a wholesale pharmaceutical outfit.

Hoby pulled the Buick around to the street behind the building. A sidewalk led from the curb across a myrtle-blanketed lawn to the back door. Hoby twisted the knob, but it wouldn't give. Slipping a credit card from his wallet, he tried to pry open the spring lock. It wouldn't budge. Hoby stood there fidgeting when the door suddenly opened, banging his shoulder. Out came a black man wearing a dark suit, white shirt, a cap with a shiny visor.

"Well, I'l be doggone!" the man declared. "It's the Toe-Main Kid! How you been, Kid?"

"Fine . . . uh . . . just fine."

"I'm Kenny, Mr. Whammers's chauffeur. Remember, I picked you up at the airport that time you come in for the press conference."

"Sure, I remember you."

"What you doin' at this end of the building? You ought to be sittin' on a throne in front."

"Hah . . . ah . . . well. I tell you, Kenny, I just got back from a big trip and I was looking for Mr. Whammers."

"He ain't here. He's gone out of town."

"Aw, darn." Hoby looked down at his hands. "I was looking forward to talking with him. I wanted to tell him about my trip."

"How'd it go?"

"Great, Kenny. Just great."

"Doggone, I'm sorry Mr. Whammers ain't here. I just come from the airport where I put him on the airplane for Palm Springs."

"Is that right?"

"Uh-huh. He gonna spend the weekend there."

Hoby looked crestfallen. "Darn, I really wanted to see him. That's a shame. You wouldn't happen to know where he's staying down there, would you?"

"Well, let me see . . ." Kenny pressed a finger against his lips. "Sumthing about an inn . . . "

"Inn? What sort of inn?"

"I can't recall the first name . . ."

"Try, Kenny. Please try. It's very important."

"Sumthin' like Ningledick . . ."

"Ningledick?"

"Inglenick," Kenny said.

"Ingleside!" Hoby shouted, "Was it the Ingleside Inn?"

"Yeah," Kenny said, his face brightening. "That's it. The Ingleside Inn in Palm Springs."

"Thanks, Kenny! Thanks a bunch."

53

Hoby had once worked as a night clerk at the Ingleside Inn. The inn, a celebrated refuge for Hollywood personalities, was located a block off Palm Canyon Drive, backed up against the foothills of the San Jacinto Mountains. Despite the tourists who flocked to Melvyn's, the restaurant on the premises, to sit in the wicker chairs and sip tequila sours, it had a low-key, intimate, tucked-away charm. Although long past its prime, the inn was still a place where a person in search of anonymity could vanish from public view. The management was cooperative; behind the bar and restaurant, carefully screened from the rear windows of Melvyn's by oleander shrubs, were a dozen bungalows with stucco walls and red-tiled roofs. In clusters of six, the bungalows were grouped around two kidney-shaped pools. Each bungalow featured a walled patio, camouflaged by masses of boungainvillaea. The rent for the bungalows wasn't cheap. The rubes in town hoping to catch a glimpse of somebody important stayed in the ordinary hotel section, located out front on Palm Canyon Drive.

Hoby drove the Buick into the employees' parking lot and stepped out. The heat was fierce; the afternoon temperature was expected to top the 115-degree mark. He'd run the Buick air conditioner at full blast all the way from Riverside; his shirt was soaked, as was the seat of his khaki pants. He pulled out the holsters and strapped them to his waist. He needed their snug, corsetting effect. He trudged through the gate and along the curving drive, past a row of gleaming Bentleys and Rolls Royces. He strolled into Melvyn's, made his way through the empty bar, emerging onto another patio. From there a path of tessellated stones led away from the restaurant.

He had no difficulty finding Whammers. The Hamburger Baron sat next to a pool, under an awning. He wasn't alone; two men lounged nearby. Big men with slick, coco-butter tans. From a distance, warped and refracted by the heat that shimmered off the concrete walkway, they looked like basking walruses.

Hoby slipped through a gap in the oleanders and eased across the grass, hands pressed against the holsters to keep them from flapping. He wasn't noticed until he was a few yards away, and then it was too late. Lamar's head shot up from the papers he was studying; his jaw tightened. Hoby ducked under the awning and settled himself in a chair in the shade.

"For some reason, my company no longer seems to please you," he said, leaning over, his eyes fixed on Lamar. There was a commotion behind him, accompanied by the whiff of protective oil. Lamar flicked his hand and shook his head, and the odor went away as the walruses returned to their towels.

Lamar pulled off his dark glasses and gave Hoby a frank, fearless stare. He wore a pair of baggy swim trunks and a natty straw hat with a generous brim. A tiny pool of sweat glistened in the cavity between his chest and stomach, below the patch of gray hair sprouting between his nipples.

"How could it," he said, "after what you did to Ralph Manning."

"Don't hand me that crap, Lamar. That was more than justified, and you know it. When I found out that Ralph was deliberately spoiling the beef, I went nuts. I think you can understand why. You sent me out to cure sick hamburger, didn't you?"

Lamar picked a Canary Island cigarillo off the table and stuck it between his teeth. "That's right, Kid," he said, hissing smoke under the awning. "I sent you out to do a job, and you did it. Magnificently. Beyond my wildest expectations."

"At the same time your faithful toady was dogging my heels, undoing everything I had done. How do you expect me to feel? Honored? Cherished? Acclaimed? Hell no, Lamar. I'm pissed. I'm pissed as hell. But then I haven't come all the way here to extract my pound of flesh. I'd like to, but your walruses would be all over me, and I've already been beat up once and found it not to my liking. I just want to know one thing, Lamar, and then I'll be on my way. Why? What's the real reason for poisoning the hamburger? Why in hell would you do something as slimy as that?"

Lamar looked at him carefully, mulling over the question of how much he should tell Hoby, how much Hoby deserved to know. The man looked frazzled and distraught; Lamar owed him the courtesy of a response. After all he had put him through, he could at least offer him that.

"Profit, of course," he replied, pursing his lips. "You do these things because you want to make money. There's another reason, too, and it has to do with power. We live in a complicated world. People and ideas intersect and overlap. It's difficult to achieve an unobstructed view of anything anymore. It's hard to look at something and say, 'This is mine . . . this belongs to me.' The world is like a wasps' nest—everything you touch has already been soiled by somebody else's spit."

He looked out reflectively at the pool.

"That's what was so incredible about Trujillo. He was a real caudillo. When he was in power he had the Dominican Republic firmly squeezed between his fingers. He knew everything that was going on. There wasn't a fly that could fart in the jungle that he didn't know the identity of. For more than thirty years, everything that happened in that country he either initiated or brought to a successful conclusion. The man had a genius for domination."

Lamar tapped the ash off his cigarillo. "So, when the opportunity arose to maybe corner the hamburger market in the Southwest as a prelude to maybe cornering it in the rest of the country, I couldn't resist. In light of all you've done for me, Kid, I have to admit that. It was too tempting. It was like the old days in Santo Domingo when Trujillo would pick up the phone and make a couple of calls and not only fix the price of Dominican sugar on the New Orleans market but determine his own cut as well. That's power, Kid, and all my life I've been bewitched by it. Never once, in all the times I saw him do that, did I ever hear him raise his voice. He didn't have to. He didn't have to get tough or play the bully. He had plenty of underlings for that. All he did was pick up the phone and speak into it or call someone into his office and have a chat with them. That's power. When you can whisper and make people jump, that's power."

"But the chemicals, Lamar. Forget the metaphysics for a moment. The chemicals you sprayed on the fields outside Hatch and Las Cruces, and the cattle that absorbed them, and the butchers who carved them up, and the children who ate them in your outlets in El Paso and Lordsburg and Douglas and Tucson . . . what about them? I realize you're a shit hole, but why would you chart such a complicated path to get what you wanted? Why didn't you have Ralph sneak into the franchises with a DDT bomb and do the damage there? Why was the process so convoluted? Why did it have to affect so many different animals and people along the way?"

"Because it involved a cycle, Kid, and the parts of the cycle are all dependent on one another. The grass feeds the cattle, which are slaughtered for their meat, which is then chopped up and dispensed to the public. That's the routine. You don't tamper with the routine unless you really want to draw suspicion onto yourself. It's easier to foul something like this at the starting point rather than down the line. In the middle especially, there are too many snoops, too many federal inspectors. Our hamburgers were designed to sour once they hit the outlet. It didn't always work that way, but that's the way we planned it."

With no breeze circulating, it was hot under the awning. Hoby glanced over his shoulder and winced at the glare that flanged off the surface of the pool.

"I'd like to hurt you, Lamar," he said softly, riveting his eyes on the object of his fury. "I'd like to make you shriek and grovel and whimper in pain. I've got a knife in my pocket, and I'd like to stick it into your heart."

If this declaration ruffled Whammers, he didn't show it. He sighed and ran a finger through the sweat pockets under each eye. "You're not the killing type, Kid," he rebutted. "No matter how you strut and bluster, you haven't got it in you. You're a healer. You like to see things grow. Look how you cured all that hamburger. That was pure voodoo. It's never been done before, and nobody will ever do it again."

The heat bore down on Hoby's shoulders like a huge, hairy paw. With no air stirring, it must have been 120 degrees in the infernal space under the awning. "I swear to you, Lamar, with all my soul, that it would give me enormous pleasure after all the grief you've caused me."

"I wish I could let you believe that, Kid. But I can't. There's more to it than that. I'm not entirely to blame for the corruption of the WhammyBurger product. Yes, I tampered with it in hopes of getting a price hike. But something else happened unrelated to my tampering that caused the problem to spin out of control."

"What was that?"

"You ever heard of a substance called PCB?"

Hoby shook his head.

"It's a deadly chemical. In large doses it can cause cancer in humans and attack the central nervous system. The chemical collects in the fat of warm-blooded animals and doesn't break down easily. Repeated exposure to PCB causes a steady buildup in the human body."

Lamar continued. "Our cattle are plagued by insects. To relieve their misery, we rub them down regularly with a mixture of lindane and toxaphrene, with a little salvage oil thrown in. About six months ago, in an economical move, we started buying salvage oil from a dealer in Roswell, New Mexico. What we didn't know was that the new oil we were using was actually a 95 percent PCB solution that's used in the installation of electrical transformers. The PCBs were absorbed through the animals' hides and into their bloodstreams. Mixed with the chemicals they had already ingested from the grass, those steers turned into time bombs. While you were away, the Food and Drug Administration launched an investigation into the matter. For several weeks it's been very hush-hush; the results are to be revealed tomorrow. I have an advance copy of the report."

He held up a sheaf of papers. "It places the blame entirely on the use of the transformer oil. None of our meddling is mentioned. We're to be fined a heavy chunk; in addition, we have to settle out of court with the people who got sick. We're also forbidden to serve hamburger in any of our outlets for two months. At the end of that time, we can reopen our doors. Not only that, but to compensate for the revenues lost during the penalty period, we'll be permitted to tack on a 15 percent surcharge to the price of our entire hamburger line. I guess you could say we got what we wanted after all. With the help of the PCB and the sympathetic understanding of the FDA, things worked out pretty well for us."

Black spots whirled across Hoby's eyes. Sweat dribbled down his spine, collecting in a sticky ring around his belt. The world worked in ways he had never really understood. For years his father had said this, and for years his father had been right. Hoby was too naive, too sweet-tempered, too idealistic. He believed people behaved according to their instincts and that those instincts were basically sound and well-intentioned. He had no conception of the lengths some people would go to exalt themselves at the expense of others.

"And don't try and go to the press with your version of the story," Whammers warned, a resolute edge to his voice, "'cause they'll have trouble believing you. Particularly in light of an accusation that it was you who put the poison into those hamburgers. And there'll be plenty of witnesses to support that accusation. Managers of various WhammyBurger outlets who, in order to keep their jobs, will agree with my version of the story. So if you want to keep intact the reputation of the legendary Ptomaine Kid—maybe the last real hero of the Old West—you'll keep your mouth shut. You can ride a long way into the sunset on the strength of those memories."

Hoby heard himself moan. He looked down at his hands and tried to turn them over, but they felt like lead weights. He couldn't wiggle a finger.

"Sorry, Kid. That's all I can say. For awhile you took people's minds off their worries and gave them hope. Personally, I think you're a hell of a guy. But your heart is too big for your brain, and you always let it do the thinking for you. You're a pigeon, Kid. An easy mark."

Under pressure of the burning heat, Hoby's bones seemed to dissolve like liquid chalk. He made an effort to rise, but a movement from one of the walruses by the pool checked him.

"Those guys," he croaked. "Who're they?"

"A couple of crushers I put to good use now and then."

"They know me, don't they?"

Lamar flicked the butt of his cigarillo into the grass. "I presume you're referring to an incident that took place in an alley in Douglas, Arizona?"

Hoby nodded.

"They were there. I sent them to break your fingers. The FDA had concluded its report, and your services were no longer needed. I figured if you kept probing and asking questions, you'd find out about the cattle. And once you found out about the cattle and the fact that you were waging a losing battle, you'd get upset. I thought I'd spare you that indignity. With both hands broken, you'd be a martyr, and people would revere you for having suffered so much for their welfare. You'd be a real hero then."

"It didn't work out that way, did it?" Hoby sneered.

"Nope. The old guy with the guitar surprised the hell out of them. It's a good thing I'm here to protect you. Otherwise, they'd smash your face so bad your own mother wouldn't recognize it."

"I'll keep the knife in my pocket then."

"That's a good idea, Kid."

Mustering the remnants of his dwindling strength, Hoby wobbled to his feet. He tottered out from under the awning into the scalding light. The effect was like a hammer blow, knocking him off balance.

"Lamar," he said, "you are a real scumbag."

"Thanks. Trujillo thought so, too."

Hoby turned and started to walk away. The flipflop of the holsters at his waist made him pause. With steady fingers, he unbuckled the holster belt and pulled it off and tossed it into the water. For a brief moment it floated on the surface like an oily black snake. Weighed down by the holsters, the belt sank toward the drain. Hoby watched it, not moving a muscle. Then he raised both hands in a meaningless gesture, turned, and walked away.

54

Tulio was up in a date palm when the Buick rattled into the orchard. He was perched at the top of a fifteen-foot ladder, bagging dates with grocery sacks to keep them from spotting when the rains came in August and September. The thought that this might be the last harvest in this orchard made him wrap the bags with special care. With any luck, this might be the best harvest ever. He loved these trees and the dates they produced. Someday he wanted to have an orchard of his own. The thought was pleasant, but he was flat-ass broke. He had a three-year-old daughter; last week his wife told him she was pregnant. Six months from now he might be running narcotics up from Mexicali, he might be picking beets, he might be fishing for corvina in the Salton Sea, he might be in jail. The orchard kept him safe from such temptations. It drew a comforting circle around his life and offered a secure place in which he could protect his family.

When he saw Hoby get out of the Buick and clump up the steps to his apartment, Tulio dropped the sacks to the ground and scurried down the ladder. Inside, he found Hoby on the bed, propped up on one elbow, staring out the same window as the creature. The creature was sitting on the air conditioner, gazing out through the break in the tamarisk pines at the Little San Bernardino Mountains. When Tulio came through the door, Hoby made no move to cover the little fellow.

"What's the matter, man? You not feeling too good?"

"That's right, Tulio." On the bed sheet by Hoby's elbow was a stack of envelopes bearing the WhammyBurger logo. Hoby fluttered the stack with his thumb.

"How did it go, hey? Did you see Mr. Whammers? Did you get a hero's welcome?"

"It didn't work out that way. It was like coming home from Vietnam. Nobody was interested."

"That bad, eh?"

"Worse, Tulio. Worse than bad. It was awful."

"I'm sorry. That's terrible news."

Hoby stared out the window. A mingled slick of sorrow and hopeless anger slogged through his veins.

"Oh . . . listen, man, I made a phone call for you this morning. I pretended I was the personal secretary of the Ptomaine Kid. I called the widow. The widow, man. I talked to her myself, personally, and made an appointment for you to drop by her home this evening at 7:00. You should have heard me, man, I was really suave and polished. You'd've been proud. I said you had just returned from a successful healing trip and that you wished to discuss the matter of the orchard with her at her earliest convenience. She said she was going out to dinner at eight but that she could see you an hour before that. She said she looked forward to having a chat with you at her hacienda in La Quinta. She wants to hear about your trip, man. She thinks you're pretty cool."

Hoby swept the envelopes bearing the WhammyBurger logo to the floor, then rolled over on his face.

"You hear me, man?"

Hoby muttered something Tulio couldn't hear.

"You got to get your face out of that pillow, man, if you want me to understand what you're saying."

Hoby looked up. His eyes were like two cloudy gray oysters. "Let me rest an hour, huh? What time is it now?"

"Four-thirty."

"Let me sleep till 5:30. Then I'll get up. You come wake me, huh?"

"Sure."

The telephone woke Hoby at 5:20. Over in his half of the duplex, Tulio tried to reach the phone before Hoby, but he was bombed. He didn't hear the phone until the third ring, and by the time he dragged his body across the living room floor, Hoby had already picked up the receiver. Tulio listened in, his drowsed consciousness titillated by the familiar voice at the other end.

" . . . trip? I called several times, wondering when you were getting in."

Hoby sounded dopey. "Got in . . . las' night."

"How'd it go? Did you handle a lot of places?"

Tulio recognized Randolph Tibbs's voice; he'd heard it often over the past three weeks. Blustery and aggressive, despite the thick-tongued accent. An I.W. Harper voice at 5:20 in the afternoon, positive and self-confident.

"Yeah . . . sure. Hit a few. Cleaned up a lotta junk."

"They paid you anything yet?"

"Paid? Yeah . . . yeah. I got a buncha envelopes here. Look like checks, mebbe."

Tulio made a face. Hoby sounded like he was doing Seconal.

"Son, I'd like to get together and talk to you about those checks. I got some ideas I'd like to kick around regarding investment possibilities. With what you're earning and what I got stashed away, we might be able to go together and lay hands on a prime piece of property, say, in Desert Hot Springs. The present owner's got to get out, and he's willing to part with the property for a kiss on the cheek. It's got great potential."

"Hunh . . . s'okay . . . yep."

"You sound bushed, son. Did I wake you up?"

"I'z napping."

"I bet that trip about did you in."

"Close to . . . "

"I know you still got your heart set on the hamburger joint down there, but maybe we can talk anyway."

"Shure."

"Maybe tonight?"

"Got an appointment t'night, Pop. Lemme give you a call t'morrow."

"First thing? This has the makings of a real sweet deal."

"Sure . . . first thing. We'll get t'gether."

55

Hoby arrived at the widow's house a few minutes before seven. Tucked deep in the La Quinta cove, backed up against the foothills, the house was shrouded with shadows. Like most houses of substance in the Coachella Valley, it looked inconspicuous from the street. Partially screened by shrubs, painted a dull white, situated at the high point of a curving driveway, it resembled a thousand other houses. The difference was inside, or rather, just outside, starting with the gigantic brass knob affixed to the stout oak door that took two hands to heave open.

The soles of Hoby's tasseled loafers glided noiselessly across the marble foyer as he followed the maid, who led him into the living room. The ceiling was high, bolstered by polished vigas. Windows stretching from floor to ceiling along the back wall offered a view of the patio and swimming pool. In one corner stood a display cabinet full of music boxes. A grand piano—a huge piece with a raised lid and sculpted legs—sat in another.

The maid walked him to the center of the room and left him there without a word. Hoby did a slow pirouette, his heel grinding into the shag carpet. He shuffled toward a glass-topped table loaded with copies of slick European fashion magazines. Hoby rounded one end and lowered himself onto an L-shaped sofa backed by thirteen embroidered pillows. Hoby counted them.

The widow was halfway across the room before Hoby looked up. She took his hand and squeezed it—a strong, mannish grip. She wore a caftan, with drooping sleeves and a hem that touched her toes. The colors, a deep rose interwoven with gold threads, caught the predominant colors in the room. As they settled on the couch, their knees within a few inches of touching, Hoby felt a dull explosion inside his stomach.

The maid brought them white wine in crystal glasses. The light from the lamps refracted through the glasses, spotting their hands with sparkling prisms. "And your trip, Mr. Tibbs. How was it?"

Her voice seemed to unfurl from the bottom of a canyon. A throaty, rumbling voice that sent chills up his spine. "Your exploits were mentioned several times on the news, and once I think I even saw some footage of you, hard at work. But how was it really? Successful I hope."

"Yes . . . yes, indeed." The words seemed to stick to the back of his throat. "We achieved everything we wanted. The staffs of all the member franchises were cooperative. The trip was a tremendous success."

Hoby blushed through the deep tan gilding his features. An outright lie, although necessary under the circumstances. The widow's presence offered no alternative. Surrounded by the magnificence of her home—

solid tokens of material success—Hoby had no recourse but to respond positively.

"Your . . . secretary said that you wished to speak to me about a personal matter."

"Yes, ma'am, that's correct. About the orchard in Indio where we . . . where I live and that you intend to sell to a developer from San Bernardino."

"The one located between Miles Avenue and Oasis Street?"

"Yes, ma'am."

"What about it?"

"Well both myself and the other fellow who lives there, Tulio Sanchez—he looks after the date trees—well, we were wondering if there might be some way you could maybe change your mind. We love that place, ma'am, and Tulio, he's done a great job taking care of it. There's no place like it. It's like paradise to us. I've lived in this valley for twenty years, and it's the garden spot for me. I hate to see it leveled and condominiums put up in its place."

He gripped the stem of the wine glass with one hand and with the other dug his fingers into his knee.

"I appreciate your feelings, Mr. Tibbs." She looked down as if to make sure the words she was about to say were lined up in the right order. "Unfortunately, the business is out of my hands. The orchard belongs to my late husband's estate, and for tax reasons I have been advised to sell it. I recognize the capable job that Mr. Sanchez has done. However, the income from the date palms does not begin to pay his salary and the taxes on the property. In the long run, I feel it is better for me, and the property, to sell it to a developer."

"But it's such a fantastic place!" Hoby protested, with more fervor than he intended. "It's like a slice of the old, agricultural California."

"I understand, Mr. Tibbs. I'm fully aware of its historical uniqueness. But the truth is, the city is not really interested in preserving the space as it exists. Indio is a growing community. New housing is in short supply. The acreage offers a prime location between Highway 111 and downtown. It's perfect for development. Plus the price the San Bernardino developers are willing to pay is . . . well, quite generous. If I didn't sell it, I would be foolish. My advisers have been after me for a couple of years to do just that. The only reason I've hung on to it so long is for sentimental reasons. My late husband worked in that orchard as a boy. His father thought it would be good for him to learn the date business, and so he spent several summers there bagging the dates and harvesting them. He loved the place as much as you do. I dare say if he were still alive he might not let it go. But he's not alive, and I am, and I have no choice but to sell it."

Her voice resonated with emotion.

"I'm sorry for the news. I know it's upsetting, But you're a well-known man, Mr. Tibbs. There are lots of places in this valley where you can live."

Hoby's mouth filled with sand. "Not like that place," he replied. "There's no place in the world like that place. If I live to be 105, I'll never find a spot like that again."

"Perhaps you might inquire in Coachella or Mecca. There are still lots of orchards down there."

"Maybe so . . . maybe so."

The interview was over. The wine was gone from their glasses. The widow had shifted her posture to the edge of the couch. They were on their feet and moving across the carpet when the front door chimed. Three people with big, booming voices flooded in. Hoby cursed softly. He wanted a moment or two more with the widow.

He heard her introduce him to her guests—two men and a woman— tall, attractive people with athletic figures and coppery tans.

"The Ptomaine Kid, is it?" one man declared, shaking Hoby's hand. "You don't say? Well, well, this certainly is a pleasure."

An indulgent smile marked his lipless mouth. Hoby felt awkward. The guests fussed over him for a few minutes, then a silence fell between them, deep and cold: the silence of social distinctions when the mechanism of good manners has played itself out. Hoby elbowed his way between them to shake the widow's hand and thank her for listening. Her grip was polite and neutral.

56

The light was fading under pressure of a gloomy purple dusk, laced with smog and sand particles creeping down Banning Pass from Los Angeles. Hoby turned onto Highway 111 and drove to Buddy Patencio's bar in downtown Indio. There, he bought a pack of Pall Malls and took a seat in a booth. He peeled off a fifty-dollar bill and ordered two shots of Old Crow. Tearing open the pack, he fired up a cig and snuffed smoke deep into his lungs. Two puffs later he knocked back one of the shots, chasing it with a slug of beer. He ordered another shot and started in. Twice Buddy Patencio came out from behind the bar to sit with him: the first time shortly after he arrived, to inquire about his trip and bemoan the fate of the orchard; the second time, four hours later, to take away his car keys and offer him a ride home. Hoby was adamant. He might be drunk, but he could still walk. Besides, the orchard was only a few blocks away.

"Then let me call Tulio so he can come get you," Buddy suggested.

"Toolyo naint 'ome," Hoby burbled. "Gone t'see his gran'fappy."

The table was littered with beer bottles and shot glasses. There were two cigarettes left in the pack. When the waitress tried to clear away the mess, Hoby snarled at her. He took pride in the litter he had generated. Several friends drifted in, several acquaintances. Hoby drank with them, they drank with Hoby. Two guys tried to coax him outside to smoke a little boo. Hoby said no. He was a booze hound; dope was bad for his health. A woman asked him to go home with her. Hoby refused, citing a serious paralytic condition below the waist, the result of wounds received in the recent war. She said she was a nurse, skilled at resuscitating traumatized organs. Hoby still refused. Tonight was a night for liquor, not for wooing.

At 1:30, after his head hit the table, Buddy Patencio picked him up like a sack of grain and bundled him into his pickup. By the time they reached the entrance to the orchard, Hoby was feeling better. He made Buddy stop so he could walk the rest of the way. Hoby pumped his hand, declaring Buddy a crusader and a champion, and staggered down the rutted lane toward the duplex. There was a certain cunning to this ploy. He knew once he got inside his half of the house and tried to pour himself a drink, he'd knock over the furniture, bringing Tulio—a light sleeper—on the run. Tulio was a pothead; alcohol was old school—he didn't approve of drunken behavior. Tucked away in the scaly bark of a date palm alongside the lane was a pint of Cabin Still. The tree, Hoby remembered fuzzily, was on the left, midway between the duplex and the street. There was a number involved as well . . . eleven . . . eleven trees in from the street.

Twice he tripped and fell on his face. The second time he rolled over and gazed up at the stars. The air was sweet and shimmery. The rutted lane was a good place to die; lying in a pool of dust, Hoby could imagine his spirit circling up through the fronds of the date palms. He struggled to his feet and lurched toward the tree, windmilling his arms, tripping over a root, falling again. Cursing, wheezing, he clawed the bark until his fingers struck glass. Cabin Still, the label read. The cap came off in a jiffy. He sank down into an irrigation ditch. The ditch wasn't deep, but it was steep enough to make him lose his footing, and for the fourth time in less than ten minutes he collapsed to the ground, keeping firm hold of the bottle. Up the other side of the ditch he pulled himself, digging in with his elbows. Hoby took a swig. A stream of hot liquor trickled down his throat. He retched and howled. The bottle slipped from his fingers.

57

Mucky water streaming over his head, splattering up his nostrils and down his throat, woke him. Hoby gasped and sputtered. "Fugger!" he cursed. "Godnab shigol fugger!" Flailing his arms, he broke free of Tulio's grasp and scuttled up the irrigation ditch.

"It's nine in the morning, Hoby!" Tulio shouted. "You got to get out of that ditch or you'll fry your brains!"

Tulio's daughter—three years old, with creamy brown legs—stood next to a date palm, staring wide-eyed at the grown man. The man's face was wet . . . his hair, his shirt, his pants. The look on his face wasn't funny, but the way he flopped around, like a frog, was very funny.

Tulio shut off the hose and dragged Hoby to the top of the ditch and laid him out. The first thing Hoby saw when he opened his eyes again was the face of Tulio's daughter, leaning over him with a curious expression.

"Lying in a ditch like a stinking wino!" Tulio barked. "What's wrong with you?"

Hoby took a bandana from Tulio and wiped his face. "Guess I drank a li'l too much,' he replied.

"There was a pint of booze in the ditch with you. I suppose you thought you needed a nightcap. Christalmighty. Where's your car, man?"

Hoby winced, then remembered. "Patencio's," he muttered.

"Buddy bring you home?"

"I guess."

"Good ole Buddy, Can you walk?"

" . . . think so . . ."

"Get on back to the house then, and get a shower and get into bed."

"I don't feel real good . . ."

"You look like something the crows shit out on a stump that the sun can't dry up. Get on over to the house. Lisa, you show the compadre where he lives, eh?"

The girl nodded and took hold of the torn and soiled knee of Hoby's Haggar slacks, the ones he had put on especially for his interview with the Widow Rodriguez.

They hobbled away. Tulio clapped the straw hat back on his head. When he hadn't seen the Buick this morning, he had grown fretful. Normally he wouldn't have given it a thought, only Hoby had been acting strange lately. He had seen Hoby drunk plenty of times, but never had he known him to spend the night in a ditch. Never had he seen him this wasted. If Tulio hadn't gone looking this morning, the vultures might already be circling. Could the strange creature Hoby kept by his bed be responsible? The weird little creature that nobody could identify?

Last night at his grandfather's house in Mecca, Tulio had showed him the Polaroid snapshots he had taken of Otis. The old man peered long and hard at the photos through his good eye. Finally he looked up and shrugged. "I don't know anything more from looking at these," he said. "I see its face and eyes. I think I know how tall it is, the color of its feathers.

But I can't tell you anything else. I've never seen anything like it before. That's all I can say."

At the steps to Hoby's half of the duplex, Lisa let go of his finger and watched him totter up to the door and disappear inside. She pressed her face against the screen. She saw the man knock over a chair and bang against the refrigerator. She saw him peel off his shirt and kick off his pants. A moment later she heard the shower. A few minutes later she saw him emerge from the bathroom with a towel around his waist and squish across the floor. His bare feet left wet marks. She remembered her mother scolding her father for doing the same thing. She saw him go into the bedroom and raise one knee up on the bed, as if getting ready to lie down. But the man did not lie down. He looked at the window next to the bed and put both hands up to his mouth. His body stiffened; his back was to her so she did not see the expression on his face. A spasm of panic and distress tore through his body, followed by a bloodcurdling cry. She ran to find her father.

58

Hoby went berserk. Even before Tulio arrived at a dead run, with Lisa toddling behind, Hoby was tearing out drawers and yanking clothes out of the closet and ripping off the bed coverings. He was in the kitchen, dashing cups and plates and saucers to the floor, when Tulio burst through the door. He shouted at Hoby, but Hoby—naked, his hair wet and stringy from the shower—didn't hear. When Tulio grabbed his arm, Hoby wheeled and launched a left hook at his head. Tulio ducked; the punch swept harmlessly through the air. Tulio clamped both of Hoby's arms in a bear clutch around his chest; he dragged the raving man across the floor, and drove him through the bedroom door. Hoby fought every step of the way, struggling to free his arms, kicking with his heels, but Tulio outweighed him by twenty pounds and spotted him four inches in height. Tulio muscled him onto the bed, threw him facedown, and rolled the mattress on top of him. He then scrambled onto the mattress, flattening the man underneath.

"You had enough? You gonna behave?" Tulio shouted, his voice hoarse and cracking.

"Yef . . ."

"'Cause if I let you up and you go wild, I'm gonna hammer your brains out. You understand?"

"Yef . . ."

At the mention of a hammer, Lisa ran outside. When she returned, the mattress was back on the bed and Hoby was lying on top of it, staring at the ceiling. She put the hammer in her father's hand. He stuck it into his belt. He was listening to the naked man and nodding in response. They didn't seem to be arguing anymore. The man on the bed had an odd expression on his face. Lisa curled her fingers around the handle of the hammer that dangled from her father's belt. If the man got up again and started making noise, she intended to hit him with it.

59

The truck bearing the WhammyBurger emblem had just roared over the wash, and the driver had downshifted to get ready for the long pull up the slope of the Pozo Redondo Mountains, when the pancake crack of a high-powered rifle rang out and the right front tire went flat. Fortunately the vehicle was only going about thirty miles an hour. When the driver felt the jolt, he eased the rig onto the wide gravel shoulder and braked it to a halt. It was 7:30 in the evening, a Wednesday in mid-June. The highway, a remote stretch in southwestern Arizona, was empty of other vehicles. The driver was a good three hours from Tucson, his destination. When he heard the crack, he knew what it was. He'd been shot at before, in Vietnam. It wasn't a sound you forgot. The man's name was Paul Kapella. He was a veteran trucker, a good union man, with eleven years of road duty under his belt.

With the truck idling on the shoulder, he kicked open the door and climbed down. The last light of the long summer day drained slowly from the sky. Paul didn't have to squat down to spot the problem—a hole the size of a fifty-cent piece, punched above the rim by a high-caliber weapon, most likely a 30.06.

Straight shooting, Paul thought, looking away from the road. There wasn't much cover out here, certainly not enough to conceal a marksman with a rifle.

Couldn't be union troubles, not this far out in the boonies. Couldn't be the competition either; they were suffering from the same bugs as WhammyBurger. He'd better get on the horn and report it and get somebody down here from Ajo to help him fix the tire.

When he got to the cab, somebody was already there. A heavy-set man with the body of a Sumo wrestler, a punched-in nose, and skin the color of wet clay. The man was holding a pistol. He shrugged apologetically as he handed the keys to Paul. "I'll tell you where to go," he said.

60

Hoby cleaned up the apartment. Contritely, with Tulio and Fiona's help. He put the bed back together, hung up the clothes, swept away the broken crockery. Then, he searched the orchard. Despite the savage heat, he searched patiently and methodically, starting with the tamarisk pines and working around the duplex, out into the irrigation ditches between the trees. He looked under the grapefruit shrubs, up and down the scaly trunks of the date palms, whistling and calling Otis's name. For three hours he did this; then, exhausted by the heat, he finally stumbled back into the duplex and fell into a restless, twitchy sleep.

He woke up an hour later to the comforting hum of the air conditioner. He took another shower, dressed, and fixed a cup of tea. Then he made a sandwich and heated up a can of soup. He tried smoking, but the taste was foul. He thought of a beer or a bloody Mary, but Tulio had removed all the booze from the premises. He drank another cup of tea.

He sat at the kitchen table, staring at the wall. He couldn't focus. The parade of images that regularly flicked through his brain had slowed to a halt. Otis was gone, as mysteriously as he had appeared. The widow was selling the orchard. His career as a hamburger healer was over. In the bedroom, lying on his back, he gazed out the window through the break in the pines at the Little San Bernardino Mountains. All Hoby could think of was to find out where Otis had gone and, if possible, to go and join him.

Tulio was all for taking legal action, for going to the media and making a stink, but Hoby was reluctant. He was weary of doing battle with the likes of Lamar G. Whammers. He was ready for something else.

The sun had slipped behind the mountains. An oily light lingered under the palm-frond canopy, giving everything—the trees, the ditches, the duplex—an eerie, malarial glow. When the automobile clattered down the lane from Oasis Street, Tulio looked up, annoyed, thinking it must be Randolph Tibbs. But the car was old, a four-door Chevrolet, dusty, battered, glutted with tarnished chrome. Hoby stood up as the car shuddered to a halt, steam curling up under the hood. Tulio didn't recognize the men who stepped out. Solid, chunky, with sloped shoulders, protuberant bellies, and severely bowed legs. One of them sported a porkpie hat. The others wore baseball caps. Their bare arms were garnished with colorful tattoos.

Hoby felt curiously relieved to see them. Even though he'd never seen them before, he seemed to know who they were.

"You want me, don't you?" he said.

"Yes," said the man in the porkpie hat.

61

In the car they traveled down the eastern shore of the Salton Sea. Hoby remained silent. He sat in the back seat, next to a beefy, taciturn fellow.

For the first hour not a word was spoken. Outside, it was completely dark. The mountains behind the Salton Sea were barely visible. In the space on the dashboard where the radio ought to have been was a gaping hole, filled with packs of cigarettes, cheap cigars, and matches. At the end of the first hour the man in the porkpie hat, who was driving, took out a fresh pack and handed it around. Hoby took one, a Camel nonfilter, and puffed eagerly. The four of them smoking at once blew out great gagging clouds of acrid smoke. Hoby's eyes watered and he coughed. Somebody cracked a window down, and the air began to clear.

Hoby didn't know who they were, and he didn't care. They spoke a queer, slushy language that sounded like a bolt of mashed potatoes being shuttled between a set of loose dentures. They had come for him, and he was on his way to wherever they were taking him. Lamar had double-crossed him, the widow had brushed him off like a fly, Otis was gone . . . Hoby had no future in the old world. Maybe it was time to look for a new one.

In Yuma, they stopped for gas and a restroom break. Hoby bought a Coke, an egg salad sandwich, and a sweet roll. Back in the stuffy car, he ate the food and drank the Coke and listened to the others talk. They were Indians, what sort he didn't know. The shape of their faces looked familiar. Large, droopy faces, with mournful eyes, cheeks like mail pouches, and flat noses. Their function in life seemed to be to sit without blinking, without acknowledging anything, without giving any indication that they were even breathing. That and smoking. They smoked incessantly—great slurping drags that streamed out their mouths and nostrils.

The food perked him up. East of Yuma he cleared his throat and asked, "You fellas mind telling me what this is all about?"

Porkpie was still driving. "We need you," he replied after a long silence. "We need you for a job."

"Hamburger?"

"Sort of."

"You got a restaurant that needs fixing?"

"It's more complicated than that," said Porkpie. "Once we get there, it will be explained."

At Gila Bend they turned south. Forty-five minutes later they rattled through Ajo. Hoby peered around. It was two in the morning. Somewhere in a little house on one of these streets, Harriet was sleeping. Alone, he hoped, pining for his company. Hoby recognized the silhouette of the copper-smelting plant, the smokestacks belching ugly fumes. Past the whitewashed church in the center of town the car bumped and jiggled, past Harvey Phelps's diner a block or two later. A single light in the kitchen lit up the interior. A lump rose in Hoby's throat. Bob had entertained there, Hoby had first met Harriet there, he had cured a mess of bad hamburger there and made a lot of people happy. Harvey Phelps had confessed a dirty secret there, which led to other confessions and the unraveling of a spool of unsavory truths. Hoby wasn't sentimental, but with the past a field of rubble and the future yawning like a void, he couldn't escape feeling a pang or two. He closed his eyes and leaned his head back in the seat.

62

Paul Kapella awoke that morning inside the wickiup to discover that he had a bunk mate. A white man, with dark curly hair and fair skin. Paul rubbed his eyes and tossed the blanket off his legs. For three days, ever since his truck had been hijacked, Paul had remained inside the wickiup. He hadn't been mistreated; he was free to move around; he was free to walk away if he wanted. Twice a day a woman brought him food, although he didn't eat much of it: crushed mesquite beans mixed with water and dried plants that tasted like old newspaper. The sight turned his stomach. He yearned for a couple of hamburgers. There were plenty of patties in the refrigerated truck parked in the shade a few hundred feet from the wickiup, but he couldn't touch them. They now belonged to the people of the Papago Nation, this branch of it anyhow, a traditional sect that lived in a hamlet south of Quijotoa, not far from the Mexican border. Unfortunately, those people weren't able to enjoy them either. The patties were tainted by the same sickness that had soured all the other hamburger in the Southwest.

On his hands and knees, stealthy as a ferret, Paul crawled over to the newcomer and peered into his face. The face looked familiar. Paul was sure he had seen it on television in Tucson. The fellow was famous. He was known throughout Arizona as the Hamburger Savior. He had magic hands and reportedly could cure any kind of sick meat.

Paul imagined a mess of burgers popping over a mesquite flame. His stomach gurgled and growled. The fellow looked tired, but Paul woke him anyway and explained who he was and what he wanted.

63

The place where Hoby had been taken was located in a long, narrow valley. A wash—muddy and flowing in the spring but dry now, caked and cracked with massive slabs of sand—meandered out of the hills between a cluster of wickiups fashioned out of mesquite and paloverde wood and thatched with weeds and palm fronds. There were maybe two dozen of these dwellings scattered along the banks of the dry river bed. An assortment of ancient trees, mainly willows and sycamores, sheltered the village from the noon light. It was a pleasant spot, tucked away in an obscure corner of the reservation, situated close to a water source, with a dirt track winding back through the hills.

Later that morning, Paul and Hoby and a Papago headman named White Hat sat under the shade of a ramada that stretched between two huts where White Hat lived with his family. Speaking slowly and distinctly, White Hat explained to Hoby why he had been brought there. A severe drought had curtailed the bean crop—pinto and mesquite and tepary beans that formed the staples of the traditional Papago diet. Deer had grown scarce; smaller animals like the peccary had disappeared. The people of the village—hardcore traditionalists who refused to accept handouts from the Bureau of Indian Affairs—were desperate for protein.

At the insistence of several young men, Paul's WhammyBurger truck had been hijacked between Ajo and Tucson on the highway that ran through the heart of the reservation. When the meat was cooked and served to the old people and children, they got sick and vomited. A couple of children went into convulsions and nearly died.

That's when Paul Kapella nearly died, too. The young warriors wanted to stake him to a hill of red ants, but White Hat and another headman named Amos intervened. It wasn't Kapella's fault, they explained. All over the Southwest, hamburger meat was putrefying for reasons best known to white people and their peculiar ways. The chiefs chided the men for acting impetuously and for not submitting their proposal to council. Now they were paying double for their foolishness. Not only had they hijacked a truck belonging to a big corporation, but the meat had turned out to be worthless. Now they had a truckload of tainted meat to dispose of.

"I suggest we send the hamburger back with the driver," White Hat said.

This was the first night after the truck had been hijacked. The headmen were meeting to discuss the problem. They were sitting around a fire outside White Hat's wickiup, smoking and staring into the flames.

Amos raised a finger and requested to be heard. A short, slight man with thin features, of part Hopi ancestry, he was respected for his sagacity and goodwill. "There is a man I know of who can cure sick hamburger," he began. "My cousin who works in the copper plant in Ajo told me about him."

"And that's how you came to be here," White Hat concluded, turning his grainy, ash-colored face toward Hoby. "Your fame is known all over the world."

Hoby stared gloomily at his pale, freckled hands. "I'll do what I can," he said.

64

As soon as the sun went down, he and Paul dumped a dozen boxloads of patties onto a canvas tarp. Everyone in the village gathered around. Two big fires were lit.

Hoby directed that all the hamburger be brought out of the truck and dumped onto the tarp. Five hundred boxes, each box containing 120 patties. It was the biggest load he had ever tackled.

The odds didn't faze him. He had a reputation to live up to. The microbes were there, glittering like bits of mica on a hillside. Awaiting his touch, his power.

Off came his shoes, shirt, pants. Stripped to his boxer shorts, he clambered up the pile. The path was gooey, and he sank down to his ankles; slogging, high-stepping, he finally reached the top.

The crowd was enthralled. A pudgy white man stood at the top of a small hill of hamburger meat, clad in a pair of boxer shorts bearing a faded plaid design. The old women giggled and hid their faces in their skirts. The reflection from the bonfires flickered off the man's pallid cheeks.

"I know you folks need this meat to warm your innards, and I'm gonna try and make it edible for you."

He fell onto the stack and commenced burrowing his way to the bottom. An hour into it, he realized that his hands had lost their zip. The task was taking longer than he expected. He had to grind his fingers across each patty a half-dozen times to eliminate the microbes. The process was exhausting. At this rate it would take a week to work his way through the stack.

At the end of the second hour, Hoby could barely pinch his fingers together. His arms and shoulders ached; the muscles along his back had knotted up. The sense of purpose he once felt had been replaced by a sense of futility. No longer was hamburger the precious substance on whose health the continuing good fortune of Western Civilization depended. To Hoby, it had become another worthless by-product, like the slag around a copper pit.

An enervating lethargy crept through his limbs. He plugged away for awhile longer, then collapsed. At approximately two hours and thirty minutes into the mission, overcome with weariness and despair, he curled up at the bottom of the hole and fell asleep.

When he didn't appear, Paul Kapella removed his shoes, crawled up the stack, and leaned down into the opening. At the bottom he thought he saw a white form, curled up in a fetal position. "Kid! Kid!" he called.

"Wha . . . hnnn . . . "

"Speak to me, Kid! What's going on?"

"Paul . . . nuthin . . . tired . . . fagged."

"Get back on the job, Kid! There are a half-million Indians out here ready to skin our nuts if you don't perform. Get cracking!"

" . . . lemme sleep . . ."

"You son of a bitch!"

Paul snatched a handful of patties and cocked his arm to hurl them into the hole. Just then the lip of the hole gave way; the sides collapsed, and the entire middle section of the big stack, with Paul hooting and raging, caved downward in a tumbling heap upon the recumbent figure of the Ptomaine Kid.

It took the Papagos several minutes to pull the two men out. Paul was in shock, his eyes gaping. Hoby was breathing, but his body had gone rigid. Amos blew smoke into his ears, mouth, and nostrils. Hoby's clenched form relaxed. Amos blew more smoke into him. Then he took a long drink from a water gourd and spit it into Hoby's face. With a sigh, Hoby came out of it; he sat up and looked around.

"What happened?" he croaked.

"The sky fell in," said White Hat. He ordered that the meat be dumped into the fires. The women volunteered, but White Hat called on the three men who had brought Hoby to the reservation to do the job.

It took the rest of the night to gather up the patties, carry them to the fires, and throw them in. Fueled by the grease and fat, the flames leaped high into the limbs of the sycamores. A mass of sticky smoke billowed up over the village, obscuring the stars. By the light of the false dawn, Porkpie picked up the last load and tossed it in. As the flames flickered up, he took off his hat and stomped it with both feet.

Amos nudged him aside and picked up the hat. He punched the crown back into shape and smoothed the brim. Then he sailed the hat into the smoke. When it emerged on the other side it was a white pigeon, wings flapping.

65

The next morning Paul Kapella walked out of the wickiup to find the remains of the poisoned hamburger smoldering on the bonfires. His eyes bugged; his complexion reddened.

"This is outrageous!" he screamed at White Hat. "Tainted or not, you had no right to dispose of the merchandise like that! That's at least $30,000 worth of hamburger you burned up. How am I going to explain that to my boss in Tucson?"

White Hat was unruffled. "We done you a favor. The hamburger was doomed. Whether it caught fire here or in Tucson don't matter. All over the Southwest the process has begun."

"What process? What are you talking about?"

"All stocks of tainted hamburger are to be destroyed. By order of the FDA, current supplies of infected hamburger are being buried or put to the torch. We saved you the trouble of finding a location in Tucson. And, 'cause you'll be riding lighter on the way home, we also saved you some gas."

"What?" Paul spluttered.

"You don't have to thank us. Just get in your truck and drive out of here. That will be thanks enough."

"Where did you hear this?" Paul roared.

"On the radio. On the television."

Paul's face was puffy with exasperation. He stomped back to the hut and shook Hoby awake. When Hoby heard the news, he put his shoes on the wrong feet and stumbled out to the campfire in front of White Hat's dwelling.

"Is it true?" he gasped.

The headman nodded.

"Then why did you let me make a fool of myself last night?"

"You didn't."

"He did, too," said Paul. "You all did. If you knew the FDA had issued the order, why didn't you say so? We nearly got ourselves killed."

Ignoring Paul, White Hat said to Hoby: "You tried to cure the hamburger. That's your job. That's the gift you were given. Had you succeeded, we could have used it. You didn't, so now we'll go back to digging irrigation ditches to water our beans."

"You still acted in a high-handed fashion," Paul blustered. "You still ought to have to pay the WhammyBurger organization."

White Hat's face stiffened. "The WhammyBurger company should pay us for disposing of its worthless merchandise," he said firmly. "I was against the heist from the beginning, but the young men were uncontrollable and acted on their own. That action has brought us nothing but grief. As far as I'm concerned, your truck should never have been allowed on our land."

Paul shot him a withering look. "Get this guy, will you? he sneered. "Holier-than-fucking-thou. Mister Mystical Redskin, whose shit doesn't stink. You make me puke. You're all a bunch of pathetic losers."

Two men, brandishing ironwood clubs, rushed forward, eager to unload on Paul, but White Hat waved them back.

"Go, Mr. Kapella. I'm sorry for the inconvenience we have caused you. For that I will apologize, But for your behavior as a human being I will make no excuses. You are a barbarian."

"How do I find my way out of this shithole?"

"See that man over there on the motorcycle? Follow him."

Paul clomped off, then turned around. "Kid, I can give you a lift into Tucson."

Hoby stared into the fire. An alarm went off in his head, warning him that whatever decision he made might be irrevocable. He was teetering on the edge of something, and if he stepped off, no lifeline could haul him back to the safety and comfort he had previously known.

"If it's okay with White Hat, I'd like to stay here awhile."

Paul screwed his face into an expression of disdain. "Well, you're a dumb fuck. That's all I got to say. You're about the dumbest white fuck I've ever known."

A few minutes later the truck engine fired up and Paul roared off. Hoby watched until the truck was out of sight and the engine could no longer be heard. Turning to White Hat, he asked, "Is that true what you said about them burning the hamburger meat?"

"All over the Southwest fires are blackening the sky. They burn for a long time, and they stink up the air. Some of our people have seen this with their own eyes. It's being covered on the television. Soon all the hamburger that you tried to heal with your hands will have vanished in the air."

A huge weight slid off Hoby's shoulders. He seemed to breathe freely again. He looked searchingly into the fire.

"I want to earn my keep," he said.

"We're digging a new canal from the well to the bean field," said White Hat. "You can start there."

66

The work was hard. His body wasn't used to that kind of labor. His hands and forearms were, but not his back and shoulders or his legs.

At first light he was out in the field hefting a pickax. There were a dozen men in the group. At noon they knocked off; after lunch and a siesta, they worked till dusk.

The first few days Hoby had to rest a lot. Tomas, the foreman, was patient. He told Hoby to work toward discovering a natural rhythm in his body.

"Once you find that rhythm," he said, "and work yourself into it, the heat and the flies and the pain won't bother you so much."

Hoby shared a wickiup with two other men. At night, before collapsing into his hammock, he could barely raise his head to swallow a little soup or a cupful of beans. Every joint and muscle ached. In the morning he was so stiff he could barely hobble out to the field. As the day warmed up, and he slowly insinuated himself into the rhythm of the pick, his muscles relaxed, the knots inside his joints dissolved.

Gradually, his body hardened. Gradually, his muscles became accustomed to the crushing labor. Gradually, he worked his way into a placid, consciousless state, devoid of chatter and distracting images. His mind became another functioning unit in the overall mechanism of his body.

Hoby was grateful for the respite from the daily barrage of images of success, fame, happiness, sexual conquest, immortality. Images of him sequined and glittery as a rock star, preening in front of an audience of worshipful admirers that included his father and the widow. Gradually, these images faded, replaced by familiar images of food and water and sleep and burning sunlight. Images of lizards and jack rabbits and birds.

They came at night, mockingbirds mostly, to perch on the edge of his dreams. At first he was intimidated and didn't respond. Then one night they took him with them, out into the desert air, under the waxy sheen of a three-quarter moon. All night he followed them, imitating their spiraling flight, marveling at their swirling whistles and trills.

As dawn touched the eastern horizon with a faint blush, the birds guided him back to the wickiup. Outside the huts, the cooking fires were crackling. Thanks, he muttered. His eyes popped open. The day rushed in, dazzling and bright.

"Thanks," he said again, outloud, and sat up in his bunk.

67

One day Harriet found him. How he didn't know. Most likely through one of the Indians who worked in the Ajo copper plant. She showed up one Friday evening as Hoby was eating a plate of rice and peppers. She looked pretty. Her curly hair was cut short. Her jeans fit snugly around her crotch. Almost a month had elapsed since Hoby had come to live with the

Papagos. It was mid-July. A lot had happened to him since he last saw her. His hands had grown calloused. His fair skin was chapped and stained by the desert sun. He spoke in a gutteral voice, punctuating his words with grunts and nods.

Harriet didn't reproach him for not telling her where he'd been. She was glad to see him. She missed his company. She ran her fingers over the taut muscles lining his chest and arms. She liked the way he looked—dark, strong, mysterious.

"It's a whole new career for me," he explained, feeling awkward and embarrassed at the sight of the woman with whom he had dallied so fiercely back in the days when he had a reputation to maintain. She looked pretty much the same—leaner, thinner, a little gaunt around the cheeks and eyes.

"I've lost weight wondering about you," she confessed. "Out in Indio they think you're dead. I talked to your friend Tulio. He misses you a lot."

"I miss him, too. But I got to stay here awhile longer."

"They're not holding you?"

"Oh, no. I can walk off any time I want."

She looked at him worriedly. "You know they still haven't gotten it out."

"Got what out?"

"You mean you don't remember?"

"Remember what?"

"The poison. In the meat. It's still there."

With her eyes and the urgency of her voice she tried to communicate the importance of her message. "The medicines, the quarantine, the spraying, the burning . . . none of them have worked. The meat is as bad as when you were working with it. Worse."

He squinted at her, trying to think of a reason why he should be upset. Usually the sound of a woman's worried voice bore through his chest like a termite through soft wood.

She should have gotten in the car and gone back to Ajo, but she didn't. She was sure she could make him understand the importance of what she was saying. She was positive that someday he would take up the crusade again, and this time she would be at his side.

68

Hoby's bunk mates didn't come back that night or the next night either, which gave Hoby and Harriet time to get reacquainted.

Hoby hadn't thought about sex for weeks. He presumed it was because he'd been working so hard. The pressure of Harriet's lips stirred his ardor. Before the sun went down, they were coupling on the mat in the corner of the wickiup, Hoby driving hard and steady, snorting like a horse into a bagful of oats.

She left the next day. He waved listlessly as the car disappeared over the hills in a funnel of dust. They both knew something had changed, although neither could say what it was. She felt as if he had drifted beyond the point where she could call him back. He was different. He looked different. His head swiveled alertly from side to side. He spoke in exaggerated syllables like a man trying to say something underwater. She cried all the way back to Ajo.

69

The evening after Harriet left, Hoby sat in his hut with White Hat, talking and smoking. The Indian told Hoby about the legends and history of his people; in return, Hoby told him about Otis. The story took a while to tell. White Hat didn't interrupt, except to roll a cigarette.

"I have never seen this creature," White Hat said. "But I have heard of it. It looks like an owl. It looks as though it ought to be able to fly, but doesn't. Few people have seen it. For you to have had it in your possession for so long is remarkable."

White Hat sniffed deeply at the smoke that curled off the tip of the cigarette.

"After the earth came into being, there were many of these creatures. They had a body like a badger, but instead of fur they were cloaked with feathers. Their talons were long and sharp; not only could they cling to trees, they could burrow holes in the ground. This creature was responsible for digging the tunnels that enabled our people to climb out from the center of the earth."

His voice was hypnotic. The rhythm of the words, the steady intonation, made their meaning clear. The words circled Hoby's head. They didn't bend or double back. There was no duplicity in their intent or meaning. They meant exactly what they were intended to mean.

"I have something for you to think about. In October, several warriors intend to take a journey. In addition to killing an enemy or capturing an eagle, there is a third way to obtain power, and that is to make the long, difficult journey by foot over the *Gran Disierto* to fetch salt from the shores of the Sea of Cortez. The journey takes four days, to the south, into the face of the sun, the direction of suffering.

"Such an ordeal has its rewards. With us it has become a ritual, a means by which young men can obtain dream power. The terrain is bleak and desolate. The sight of the Sea of Cortez is enough to bring the penitent into contact with the supernatural. Another function of the journey is to gather salt pellets to scatter on our fields. The pellets attract moisture. They are like corn.

"You are not Papago, so what does this mean to you? Since you are looking for something in your life more satisfying than self-glory, the Salt March might offer you a way to find it. The fact that the creature singled you out makes you different. The creature is an instrument of change. It does not mean what you think it does. You are not meant to cure bad hamburger meat. You are meant to realize a different destiny than you ever imagined.

"Think about it. If you would like to go, you are welcome. We are pleased with the way you have adapted to our life. You helped us when we were in need. Now maybe we can help you."

70

There were six in the party: Hoby, four young Papago men, and the subchief Amos, who had made the trip before. Amos was older than Hoby—nobody knew how old. He had the vigor of a man half his age. Small, fine-boned, with thin features and swarthy skin, he looked different from the beefy, slope-shouldered Papagos. In fact, he was only part Papago; the other part was Hopi, legendary desert sojourners. Amos was a medicine man, gifted and wise. The Papago were delighted to have him along. Things rarely went wrong when Amos was in charge. His dream life was potent.

The day the sun passed over the equator, Amos met with the penitents to tell them about the journey. They would talk among themselves in a special language, a lexicon of abstract phrases Amos referred to as "soft words." It would be dangerous for them to mention in plain terms the sun, the coyote, the drinking gourds, the sea. They would be too close to the nexus of power in the Papago cosmos to venture such familiarity, so instead they would refer to them as "the shining traveler," "the burning-eyed comrade," "the round objects," and "where everything is wet."

They would wear loincloths and sandals. They would carry nets for the salt pellets. Each man would carry cornmeal in a pouch and a gourd water bottle. They would walk single file. As they walked, Amos would sing songs to ease their thirst and fatigue.

Between the village and the sea there were three water holes. Many Spanish explorers had perished from not knowing the exact location of these water holes. The first two had to be reached at the end of the first two days. However, no one should drink from them until Amos said they could. Eagle down must first be sprinkled on the water and a prayer offered to the spirits. Only then could they replenish their gourds. Only then could they eat their cornmeal.

71

The time came. Mid-October. Time of early evenings and lengthening shadows. The sun, in its house on the other side of the equator, burned bright but not too hot. Many birds had migrated. Coyotes milled about. Lizards looked for holes in which to retire. In September it rained — the monsoon season, fat clouds billowing up from Mexico. To invigorate the all-important bean crop, it needed to rain some more.

They left at dawn, the sky streaked with pink rays. Amos led the way down the riverbed, past the well, the irrigation ditch, the bean field. The others followed, single file. Hoby was midway along the line, a gourd strapped to his hip, his crotch bound in a cloth strip, wearing sandals, an empty net strung across his bare back. Walking was easy at first, across arid, undulating terrain, stubbled with mesquite and creosote. After awhile they fell into a rhythmic cadence—shoulders canted forward, hands dangling—an easy lope Amos had taught them.

By midmorning the air began to warm. Sweat dappled their pores, their breath came in staccato gasps; the little gear they carried grew sweaty and cumbersome. At midday Amos paused under a smoke tree to refresh himself from his water gourd. During the hour in which they rested, the sun reached its apogee and began to slide to the horizon.

Hoby was winded. His legs were hard, his belly flat. Every day for the past two months he'd hiked five miles or more, not only to accustom his body to the physical ordeal that lay ahead but also to condition his mind to the spectacle of all that distance, all that space. As the first day progressed, he fell into an easy stride, accompanied by a murmurous chant Amos had taught him.

In the scorching afternoon they started again. The path was more difficult, up and over a series of low, scrub-covered hills. Other than the labored rasp of their breathing and the crunch of their sandals against the hard sand, there was no sound. Amos had warned them to keep in the path of his footsteps, lest they veer off the trail and damage a nesting site. No use on such a perilous journey to make anyone angry, not even a stinkbug or an ant.

By mid-afternoon the sun flooded the sky and surrounding terrain until Hoby could see only the dark, glistening scalp of the man directly ahead of him. His bare skin burned from the heat. Amos swabbed his back and shoulders with oil from the jojoba bean. An eagle soared overhead in an expansive gyre, waiting, watching.

Before sundown they reached the first water hole. No one swigged from his gourd until Amos scattered an offering of eagle down onto the brackish surface and gave the men permission to drink.

That night, after a meager repast of cornmeal, they laid down at the foot of a live oak, their heads pointing south toward the sea so their minds might become more susceptible to its enchantment. Amos intoned a prayer to the clumps of salt waiting on the shore, telling them to be patient, that they would soon be there to collect them. Stick taps on the bottom of his drinking gourd provided a haunting accompaniment. Amos's voice sounded flat and monotonous. As the prayer progressed, however, Hoby was able to distinguish variations. Each rambling supplication opened on a raw, grating note that gradually smoothed out as it rose higher. Approaching the magic part, Amos expelled the words singly, spitting each syllable out like a pellet. This went on for some time, the words erupting distinctly, enveloped in separate puffs of air; then his voice faded and died away.

That night, as they slept, a breeze murmured through the branches of the live oak.

72

The morning of the second day the trail grew steep. The sun blazed down. Mirages congealed in the clarified air—flapping pennants atop fortresses with crenellated towers; soldiers in glinting armor, their faces hooded with steel visors; priests in tattered surplices, clutching sheets of Scripture; bandits carrying bags of leafy plants; wailing women in widows' weeds; wild pigs scarfing the entrails of slain *federales*. Hoby took it all in stride. Images of suffering inspired by the wretched terrain. It happened to anyone who tried to resist the lure of this desolate blight, who tried to recloak the blight in alien niceties. No sword or cross or flourishing pen could subdue this country. All efforts to make it palatable were doomed. Survival depended upon doing exactly as the land instructed: back off, hunker down, remain quiet, stay still, breathe shallowly. Hoby was learning.

That night he lay with his head pointing to the sea and listened to Amos's ululations until his eyes closed and sleep relieved him of the pains of the day.

Mid-afternoon of the third day they reached the third water hole at the foot of *Mount Piñacate*, a fearsome peak of twisted magma and petrified volcanic ash. Before they could replenish their empty gourds, Amos ordered them to climb to the top of the peak and make an offering of eagle down in the direction of the sea.

Hoby lagged behind. His eyes bugged. His lungs wheezed. At the summit, he had to lie down until his legs stopped trembling. In the distance the blue waters of the Sea of Cortez sparkled in the sunlight. The sight invigorated Hoby. He stood on his toes and stretched out his moist fingers. The wind scattered the eagle down off the summit in the direction of the water.

The next morning, the fourth day of the journey, the penitents reached the sand flats where the autumn tides had stranded pools of salty water. Several had evaporated, leaving a rubbly scree of saline crystals. Before the crystals could be harvested, Amos plunged a stick coated with eagle down into the salt field. "O dried waters," he called, "we come not to harm you. We come only to gather your corn . . ."

He ordered the others to trot around the salt bed four times. Then he made them pray. At last they were free to fill their nets with crystals. As each man stooped to his labor, he recited, as instructed, "We take you because we need you. Be light now. Do not weigh heavy. We must carry you all the way home . . . "

With the salt gathered, they formed a line and marched into the sea, strewing crystals upon the waves. Amos waited onshore, sitting next to a fire, singing at the top of his voice. Holding the crystals in their left hands and scattering them with their right, the men advanced in a shuffling line out from the shore. The water lapped at their waists, chests, and necks.

Amos warned them that if they carried evil thoughts, the sea would reject their offering. But if they wished to live wisely and generously the corn would sink, seeding the water with fresh rain.

A flock of white-winged gulls thrashed through the air. Hoby felt himself rising free of the sand. A stingray slipped under his feet, whisking him out to sea, past schools of basking albacore and yellowtail, into an ancient crack runneling the watery floor. Clouds of muck and silt engulfed him. He splashed wildly, trying to get his bearings. With ecstatic overarm sweeps, he swam back to shore.

He was the last man to straggle in. Amos fed him like a mother pelican, pulling masticated slugs out of his mouth and sticking them in Hoby's. Hoby collapsed by the fire and fell into a dreamless sleep.

In the dark hours before dawn Amos woke them, and they started back on the long trail. As on the journey out, they had to make each of the water holes by nightfall. Because they were in a holy state, they maintained a distance of several yards between one another lest their powers clash. They were forbidden to touch their bodies with their hands. Before starting out, Amos handed each man a stick with which to scratch his parched skin. They were told not to look over their shoulders at the sea. "Do not speak to each other," Amos counseled. "Only speak to me."

It wasn't until they were well past *Mount Piñacate* that Hoby realized he had undergone a radical transformation. His body had shrunk in size, the bones and muscles had tightened, tough callouses cobbled the soles of his feet.

He moved across the sand like a lizard.

73

Harriet was in his wickiup when he returned to the village with the others. They arrived shortly after dark, panting feverishly, gulping for air; the dogs heard them coming but refrained from barking. At first she couldn't single him out from the others. They were tired and sweaty and covered with dust and sand. Hoby stood by the fire drinking water. Harriet crept toward him. Which one is he? she wondered. In the flicker of orange flames, they all looked the same. Hoby saw her first. His eyes protruded from their sockets like polished stones. "Hoby?" she called.

It took her a few moments to realize who he was. She screamed and kept screaming until she fainted. When she came to, she started screaming again. Hoby poured tiswin down her throat. She cackled and giggled and cackled some more. She had expected a change, but not like this. She felt betrayed. Hoby had two-timed her. He had misrepresented the purpose of the Salt March to her. He had told her it was for his mind, to help put the confusing events of the past six months into perspective. He had not said anything about a possible physical change. "What's happened to you?" she asked. "What have you become?"

He didn't know. When he tried to explain, the words made no sense. It was as if he no longer spoke a language common to both of them.

He seemed fine with it. It was what he had wanted ever since he had elected to remain in the village and not leave with Paul Kapella. For Harriet the change was appalling, and she screamed as she confronted him at the fire in the center of the village.

Everything about him had changed except his hands. He looked like a Papago; he was short and squat, with bowed legs and stocky shoulders. His face was broad and thick, his nose flat, the nostrils flaring. His hair had lost its curl and lay across his skull like a coarse thatch. His chest was stout, his arms long and corded with muscle. His hands, though, were still white and delicate, the fingers pudgy and moist. The hands of a shopkeeper, a recorder of deeds and events. The hands of a hamburger healer.

Amos calmed her down with a potion. She slept in the wickiup for a few hours, with Hoby squatting on his haunches next to her, fanning her with a palm leaf. He didn't understand what all the fuss was about. Granted, he had changed; he was aware of that. But wasn't that what he wanted?

Harriet left the next day in her car to return to Ajo. Hoby walked her to the driver's side and opened the door. He said nothing to her as she started the engine. Tears streaked her face; her mouth flared in a stricken grimace. He didn't wave as she guided the car out of the village.

He was determined that the transformation be complete. He had come too far to be disappointed by a detail like his hands. A week after returning from the Salt March, he sat with Amos and White Hat under the shade of the ramada. They suggested that Hoby go back to the place where he had first seen Otis.

"Go there on foot," Amos said. "Pick your way through the canyon and up the slope to the *piñon* tree where you first saw the creature. And then pray. Pray with all your might. I don't know what will happen. Maybe something, maybe nothing."

74

Hoby took a bus to Indio early one morning in the first week of November. From the bus station he walked to Highway 111 and hitched a ride to Palm Desert. He found a motel room and slept all day. That evening he strapped the cornmeal pouch around his waist and slung the water gourd around his neck. Walking the streets he looked like any other *bracero*—short, swarthy, invisible to the Anglos hurrying by in their Lincolns and Cadillacs—except that he walked fast and his feet made hardly a sound. He proceeded along Portola Avenue toward the foothills of the Santa Rosas. Over the wire fence of the UC Research Laboratory he slithered, passing through a flock of bighorn sheep, which scattered at his approach. Then into the mouth of Deep Canyon, a torturous fissure that snaked its way between the foothills to the base of the Santa Rosa Mountains. All night under the sliver of a new moon, he picked his way along the canyon floor. Mostly he followed a dry bed, the path occasionally blocked by rocks and boulders that had tumbled down the steep slopes. Over these obstructions he clambered, plugging away, making progress. At daybreak he reached the spot where the canyon split into two smaller canyons. Eight hundred feet over his head, at the top of the canyon wall, was the turnout from the highway and the pinon tree where he had first encountered Otis. Scrunched between two boulders, comforted by their warmth, he rested in the canyon for the entire day.

At dusk he started up. Hand over hand, rock to rock, up a severe incline that six months ago he would never have attempted. Through dense growths of manzanita he wiggled, aided by the light of the fledgling moon. Owls remarked upon his presence. Nighthawks chased after insects. Midway along, he startled a deer and sent it plummeting through the brush. Around midnight, his face glistening, his fingers torn by thorns, he pulled himself up on the ledge. He had to wait until a teenage couple finished coupling and rolled up their blanket. As soon as the car turned out on the highway, Hoby squatted down under the *piñon* tree.

75

In the Indio bus station Hoby had read the *Los Angeles Times*. The hamburger industry was in shambles. The poison scandal had hit the front page right after Labor Day and two months later it was still making headlines. The FDA ordered the closing of all hamburger parlors from Los Angeles to San Antonio. Despite the wholesale incineration of tainted hamburger, the epidemic could not be brought under control. The feds didn't know who to finger. The blame appeared to reside in the indiscriminate use of PCB as an insect repellent for cattle. Contributing factors were suspected; the feds weren't sure who or what they were. They were investigating.

Meanwhile, Lamar Whammers had announced that his company was on the verge of perfecting a totally synthetic hamburger made of nonmeat products that would have the same flavor and taste as hamburger, but would contain no harmful microbes.

An editorial in the same paper questioned the whereabouts of the Ptomaine Kid. Missing since last July, he had been the object of an intensive four-state search. Foul play was suspected. One rumor indicated he was in hiding on an Indian reservation in Arizona, although the rumor could not be substantiated. "Where is he," the editorial lamented, "when we most need him? A talent like that should be put to work. The people need their hamburger. They can't live without it. And the Ptomaine Kid is most likely the only person who can restore it to them."

But the Kid had dropped out; he was in retirement, self-exile from the concerns of the hamburger world. He was sitting under a pinon tree in the Santa Rosa Mountains, emptying himself of personal thoughts and feelings, making himself over into a suitable vessel for magic. Chanting, praying, singing, prostrating himself, dismantling his ego stick by stick, making his mind and body more susceptible to the ministrations of a power ineluctably greater than his own.

It was cold that night. The wind tore through the *piñon* tree, showering needles to the ground. Hoby never moved. He remained perfectly still, legs crossed, back straight, staring east over the canyon, over the foothills. After midnight his pulse dropped to the level of a hibernating bear. A soothing numbness spread through his body. The last remnants of self-craving slipped out through the chilly holes the wind spiked in his flesh.

When the first rays of dawn touched his cheeks, he was still sitting crosslegged in the same position. His joints ached, but the pain was tolerable. He stared boldly into the fiery orb of the rising sun. His eyes were round and luminous, his body radiant and weightless. Slowly, as the morning light lit up his face and chest, he raised his arms in salutation. His white hands had disappeared, and in their place were ten gnarled and sinewy dark-skinned fingers.